paradise and other stories

Also by Khushwant Singh

Fiction

Delhi: A Novel
The Company of Women
Burial at Sea
I Shall Not Hear the Nightingale
The Collected Novels

Non-fiction

Truth, Love and a Little Malice: An Autobiography
The End of India
Ranjit Singh: Maharaja of the Punjab
Hymns of the Gurus (Trans.)
Rehras: Evensong (Trans. with Reema Anand)
Khushwant Singh's Big Fat Joke Book
Khushwant Singh's Big Book of Malice
Khushwant Singh's Book of Unforgettable Women
The Vintage Sardar
Notes on the Great Indian Circus
City Improbable: Writings on Delhi (Ed.)

paradise
and other stories

khushwant singh

PENGUIN
VIKING
in association with
RAVI DAYAL *Publisher*

VIKING
Published by the Penguin Group
Penguin Books India Pvt Ltd, 11 Community Centre, Panchsheel Park,
New Delhi 110 017, India
Penguin Group (USA) Inc., 375 Hudson Street, New York,
New York 10014, USA
Penguin Group (Canada), 10 Alcorn Avenue, Toronto, Ontario,
Canada M4V 3B2 (a division of Pearson Penguin Canada Inc.)
Penguin Books Ltd, 80 Strand, London WC2R 0RL, England
Penguin Ireland, 25 St Stephen's Green, Dublin 2, Ireland
(a division of Penguin Books Ltd)
Penguin Group (Australia), 250 Camberwell Road, Camberwell,
Victoria 3124, Australia (a division of Pearson Australia Group Pty Ltd)
Penguin Group (NZ), cnr Airborne and Rosedale Roads, Albany,
Auckland 1310, New Zealand (a division of Pearson New Zealand Ltd)
Penguin Group (South Africa) (Pty) Ltd, 24 Sturdee Avenue, Rosebank,
Johannesburg 2196, South Africa

Penguin Books Ltd, Registered Offices: 80 Strand, London WC2R 0RL,
England

First published in Viking by Penguin Books India and
Ravi Dayal Publisher 2004

Copyright © Khushwant Singh 2004

All rights reserved

10 9 8 7 6 5 4 3 2 1

Typeset in *Sabon Roman* by SŪRYA, New Delhi

Printed at Chaman Offset Printer New Delhi

This is a work of fiction. Names, characters, places and incidents are either the product of the author's imagination or are used fictitiously and any resemblance to any actual person, living or dead, events or locales is entirely coincidental.

This book is sold subject to the condition that it shall not, by way of trade or otherwise, be lent, resold, hired out, or otherwise circulated without the publisher's prior written consent in any form of binding or cover other than that in which it is published and without a similar condition including this condition being imposed on the subsequent purchaser and without limiting the rights under copyright reserved above, no part of this publication may be reproduced, stored in or introduced into a retrieval system, or transmitted in any form or by any means (electronic, mechanical, photocopying, recording or otherwise), without the prior written permission of both the copyright owner and the above-mentioned publisher of this book.

To Naina,
the apple of my eye

contents

author's note	ix
paradise	1
life's horoscope	44
zora singh	109
wanted: a son	151
the mulberry tree	192

author's note

In 1962 Indian astrologers, without a single exception, forecast the end of life on earth on 3 February at 5.30 p.m. because at that precise moment eight planets would be in conjunction (*ashtagraha*). Tonnes of ghee were burnt in *havan kunds* midst the chanting of prayers. Schools and colleges remained closed; buses, trains and planes went empty. People stayed in their homes to be together, awaiting the apocalypse (*pralaya*).

February 3rd came and went. Nothing happened. The rest of the world laughed at us.

I hoped this experience would finally rid Indians of belief in astrology and other equally ridiculous methods of forecasting the future—palmistry, numerology, gemology, tarot cards and whatnot. My hopes were belied. There was a resurgence of

author's note

belief in the occult, together with an upsurge of bigotry and intolerance. Exaggerated piety became a façade for personal advancement. India steadily declined to become a nation of humbugs and hypocrites.

I began writing these stories two years ago, when my cup of patience with irrationality and self-righteousness was full to the brim.

paradise

Pune, 1982

What brought me here is partly recorded in my 'Dear Diary', a blue leather-bound notebook in which I put down my day's activities and thoughts right through high school and the two years I was in college. Then I felt it was a bit childish, and in any case, what I did after I grew out of my teens was not worth recording. Most of them were wasted years. I am now thirty, still single and American—at least that is what my passport says. But things have changed enough for me to want to return to my diary. The wasted years are well and truly behind me. And I am where I should have been in the formative years of my life—India.

I am the second child and the only daughter of my parents. My father is a Jew, my mother, ten years younger than he, is a High Church Anglican. Neither was particular about his or her faith. There was a *mezuzah* by the entrance of our large apartment and a *menorah* on the mantelpiece of our sitting room. Once a year, on Yom Kippur, we accompanied our father to the synagogue and my mother bought meat from a kosher butcher. And once a year we went to mass on Christmas Eve with our mother, put up a Christmas tree in our living room and had friends over for drinks, roast turkey and Christmas pudding. As far as religion was concerned, that was about all we did about it.

My father was a big-built man of Polish descent. He spoke English with a guttural, American accent. My mother was of genteel ancestry. She was small and extremely attractive, with golden brown hair, dark blue eyes and boobs to die for. Why she agreed to marry my father, who was a coarse man, I was never able to understand. He was the chief sales manager of a large, Jewish-owned department store; she the personal secretary of a member of the Board of Directors who wanted her to be his mistress. The man hounded her, so she told him where to get off and became the secretary of another member of the Board. She also agreed to marry my father who had been making passes at her for a long time.

It was a bad match from the start. My father was a philanderer. He was often away from New York on business and thought nothing of laying women willing to be laid. There were plenty of them wherever he went. He was also careless and left evidence of his philandering on the lapels of his coats and in his pockets. There were angry quarrels every time he came home. By the time I was four years old, my parents' marriage was all but over. They hardly spoke to each other. He continued womanizing; my mother found lovers. Ultimately she sued for divorce, got the apartment, custody of both her children and a hefty alimony. My father moved out and my mother began entertaining her lovers in our home.

I take after both my parents. Like my father, I'm tall; I inherited my mother's golden brown hair, her dark blue eyes and her big bust. I was voted the best-looking girl in school and was greatly sought after by the boys. I was sixteen when I lost my virginity to the captain of the school baseball team. We continued dating each other for a few months. Then he found other girls to take out and I was happy dating other boys.

So it went on through high school and college, where I did a secretarial course. I landed a well-paid job as the secretary of the owner of a publishing house. I could afford to rent an apartment of my own, but for some reason carried on living with my mother. My brother had by then passed out of college and got a job in Chicago. My mother continued entertaining her gentleman friends as and when she wanted. I went my way, inviting my boyfriends over for the night. My mother and I never got in each other's way. There were times when she had her friends in her part of the apartment and I had my friends in mine. When we ran into each other in the kitchen while getting some beer or coffee or something to eat, she would ask, 'Howya doin', hon?' I would reply, 'Fine,' and we'd return to our respective friends.

I started drinking while I was still at high school. Later, I did crack and smoked pot. I was often high and didn't even know the boys I ended up sleeping with. At times there would be six of us, drinking and smoking pot together. We'd shed our clothes and take turns having sex with different partners. This was usually on Saturday evenings so we had Sunday to shake off the effects of the booze and drugs. This went on for some years till I started feeling an emptiness inside. My enthusiasm for partying began to wane. I started hating myself for my indulgences and for making my body available to anyone who wanted it. I often went into depression. At times I contemplated suicide.

Then an incident finally convinced me that I should change my way of living or else I would go crazy.

I was alone in my part of the apartment one evening, reading in bed. My mother had a boyfriend visiting her. Their voices got louder and louder; I heard my mother shout, 'Get the hell out of my house or I'll call the police!' Seconds later a stocky, middle-aged man with bloodshot eyes staggered into my room, pulled down his trousers and held out his erect penis at me. 'Want my dick in your pussy, darlin'?' he said coming towards me. 'Your Ma is mad at me and won't have any of it. So—' Before he could take another step I flung my book at his crotch and screamed, 'Get out, you fucking bastard or I'll strangle you with my bare hands!' The book hit him on his balls. He doubled up in pain and stumbled out yelling, 'Fucking whores! I'll teach you both a lesson soon!' I bolted my bedroom door and went back to bed but I couldn't sleep. I knew that if I didn't put an end to this sort of lifestyle, it would be the end of me.

It was around then that I discovered India. I don't remember exactly how it happened except that one of my girlfriends told me that she had been to attend a few lectures delivered by some swami or the other at the Ramakrishna Centre, which was a few blocks away from where I lived in Manhattan. She had been very impressed with the speaker, and I asked her to take me with her the next time she went.

It was a large room with about a hundred chairs. Almost half the audience were Indians, the rest Caucasians of different nationalities, including Americans. It was unlike any religious gathering I had attended. The platform was bare except for a white cotton sheet spread over a carpet and an incense burner sending up spirals of fragrant smoke. A young man dressed in white shirt and pyjamas came in. He had close-cropped hair and looked clean as though he had just had his bath. He greeted us by joining the palms of his hands and with a slight bow said, '*Namastey.*' Some of the audience responded with 'Namastey'.

paradise

The man sat down on the white sheet in the lotus position and closed his eyes. He sat still for a while, then raised his hands and in a deep, resonant voice chanted, 'Om.' Many in the audience joined him. It was not a short, two-letter word they chanted but a prolonged A-U-M that echoed through the hall. I did not know what it meant but I found it very soothing.

'Friends,' he began, 'in this series of lectures you have heard me talk on various subjects. This evening I will talk about the way Hindus look at life. The Westerner views life very differently. Here you are motivated to achieve material success, which is seen as the ultimate aim of existence. You are fiercely competitive, you work very hard so that creature comforts last you till the end of your lives. Your lives are filled with tension, and many of you consult psychiatrists to help you cope with stress. You try to drown your worries in high living—drinking, taking drugs and indulging in promiscuous sex. You think high living and having fun is the be all and end all of existence. But soon you begin to feel empty inside and begin to question yourself, "Is this all that life on earth was meant to be?"'

The man's words touched me deeply. It was as

if he had been reading my mind. He had used almost the same words I used when I reflected on my own life. He continued, 'My friends, there is a bit more to life than making money and having a good time. To find the purpose of life, you have to look within yourself. Ask yourself, why was I born? What is this world all about? Where will I go after I die? Ponder over these questions in silence and in solitude, meditate on them after emptying your mind of all thoughts. The truth is within you. God is within you.' I did not understand all that he said but it set me thinking. Somehow partying, drinking, smoking pot and sleeping around didn't seem that much fun any more. I felt more disturbed than I already was. I made it a point to attend all the lectures at the Centre, where I got to know some Indians. I asked them about meditation centres in their country. They told me about ashrams, where men and women lived in communes, prayed and meditated together. Drinking, smoking and sex were taboo there. The food was vegetarian, as killing animals was regarded a sin. It was the spartan existence which intrigued me. I wanted to try it out, at least for a month or two.

The Ramakrishna Centre had many branches in

paradise

India, but these were more into social work than meditation. Indians I befriended suggested different ashrams—the Aurobindo Ashram in Pondicherry, Sai Baba's ashram in Puttaparti, the Osho Commune in Pune, the Radha Soamis' in Punjab and a number of other places along the Ganga. I wrote to many of them and received printed brochures with their terms and conditions. The board and lodging was very cheap by American standards, no more than five dollars a day. I looked up the Indian map to locate exactly where these places were before deciding on Vaikunth Dhaam in the Himalayas, along the western bank of the Ganga near Haridwar. I liked the name Vaikunth Dhaam, earthly paradise. I liked its picture in the catalogue they sent me: a small temple with a large courtyard around which ran a verandah with rooms for residents, a large meditation hall and a dining room with a long table and wooden benches. But what I liked most was what they had written against 'cost of stay'. It said, *Give as much as you like or as little as you can afford*.

My mind was made up. I told my mother I was going on a two-month vacation to India.

'Why India of all places, for Christ's sake?' she

asked. 'Full of beggars and all kinds of diseases and weird people.'.

'It has something no other country in the world has. If I don't find it I'll be back sooner,' I replied.

I bought myself an English-Hindi dictionary and learnt a few Hindi words and phrases to get by. Wanting to get a taste of the country before I got there I decided to fly Air India, New York-London-Delhi. At Kennedy Airport, I had to join a long line of Indians at the economy class counter. A man at the desk spotted me, took me from the end of the queue to the counter, checked in my valise and gave me a boarding pass. 'Madam, the economy class is full; we are upgrading you to the business class. Have a pleasant flight.' It paid to be White and blonde among browns and Blacks.

The halt at Heathrow was spent in the swanky Maharajah's lounge, being served breakfast and strolling around the shopping arcades. A new lot of passengers joined the flight to Delhi, and I got talking to some of them. They were curious to know what I was going to do in India. When I said 'Nothing, just be by myself and meditate on the purpose of life', word got around in the aircraft and I became the subject of discussion. One of the

paradise

passengers, who was from Dehra Dun, came over to talk to me.

'I've never been to Vaikunth Dhaam but I've heard a lot about it. It's not very far from where I live. I'm told it's a very beautiful ashram in the mountains through which the Ganga flows. The person who heads the ashram is said to be a very learned man. He maintains a strict discipline of daily prayer and meditation. How will you be going there?'

'Train? Bus, car? I have no idea. I'll find out from a travel agent at the hotel where I plan on staying three or four days,' I replied.

'I can tell you right now,' the man said. 'In Delhi, hire a taxi. It will take you five hours to get to Haridwar. After that you go along the Ganga on a road winding through the hills. In two hours you will reach Vaikunth Dhaam. Leave Delhi early morning, you will reach your destination by the afternoon. The taxi should not cost you more than two thousand rupees.'

I made a quick conversion into dollars. It was well within my budget. I had already paid my travel agent for three days at Le Meridien hotel.

I had heard many nasty things about immigration,

customs and cabs at New Delhi's international airport. But I had no problems at all. An Air India official took me past the immigration queue, had my visa stamped, took me and my valise through the 'Nothing to Declare' green channel and handed me over to my co-passenger from Dehra Dun who had promised to drop me off at Le Meridien in his car. Nothing could have been a smoother or pleasanter welcome to a strange country. We had landed a little after midnight; two hours later I was fast asleep in a well-air-conditioned hotel room with the 'Do not disturb' sign hanging on my door.

I do not know how long I slept. My watch still showed New York time. When I awoke, it was broad daylight outside. I thought I should let my mother know I had arrived safely. When the hotel operator connected me, I heard my mother growl, 'Oos that?'

'It's me, Mom. I'm in Delhi.'

'Is this any time to call?' she barked back. 'It's 2 a.m. for Chrissake!'

'Sorry, Mom. It's mid-morning here. Go back to sleep.' She slammed the phone down. It didn't look like she was missing me at all.

My hotel room was much the same as any good

paradise

hotel room anywhere in America. The bathroom had several little bottles of shampoos, toothbrushes, a tube of toothpaste and even a shaving kit. There was a paper ribbon around the toilet seat. There were pictures of the the Swiss Alps hanging in the room and a Gideon Bible on the bedside table. This was nothing like the India I had expected to find. I took a quick shower, changed into fresh clothes and stepped out to get something to eat—breakfast, lunch, I was not sure which. I went down to the reception and discovered it was past midday. So I had soup, a sandwich and coffee in the coffee shop. Then I walked around the shopping arcade: jewellery, carpets, shawls, antiques, drugstores. I took the elevator to the top floor where there was a large bar and restaurant. Through the massive windows I got a panoramic view of the city, from what looked like the Arc de Triomphe in Paris (they called it India Gate) up a broad avenue lined with flowering trees and a succession of water tanks to the secretariat and the Presidential Palace, which my guide book told me was called Rashtrapati Bhavan. It reminded me of Capitol Hill in Washington. Rows of cars, buses, cabs and three-wheelers, which I had never seen before, crawled along the roads in both directions. Delhi was neat and orderly and, from where I stood, noiseless. This was certainly not the India I had visualized.

I got closer to the real picture when I joined a party of tourists doing a round of the city sights in an air-conditioned bus. We drove past many old monuments and through noisy, crowded bazaars. I had never seen so many people anywhere before. Everywhere I looked there were people and more people. This was more like the India I had imagined.

I spent another two days strolling about Delhi on foot. I was pursued by beggars wherever I went. As advised by friends, I refused to give them anything. I was jostled on crowded pavements, and twice somebody felt up my bottom. I had been warned about bottom-pinchers and bag-snatchers. While I clung to my handbag, I couldn't protect my bum. It did not upset me too much. I felt it brought me closer to the real India.

On 1 March 1980, at around seven in the morning, I left Delhi for Vaikunth Dhaam. My driver was a young Sikh in a multicoloured turban. He could speak a smattering of English and was inclined to be slightly oversmart. I put him in his place right at the start of the journey. 'Keep your

paradise

eyes on the road,' I told him. 'If there is anything I want to know, I'll ask you. I don't like talking very much.'

'Right, Madam,' he replied. 'We make one stop, halfway to Haridwar. Madam can have hot cup of coffee. I will have short break.'

So it was. We drove out of Delhi through nondescript, shabby towns. There was heavy traffic—cars, buses, tractors, bullock carts, bicycles—the driver kept blaring his horn. The little that I saw of the countryside did not impress me: it was flat as a pancake with patches of green wheat and mango orchards, dustier than anywhere I had ever been. We had the windows rolled up and the air-conditioner on to shut out the dust and the noise. I didn't bother to ask him the names of the towns we passed, as they wouldn't have meant anything to me. Two-and-a-half hours later we pulled into the parking lot of a fast-food eatery called Cheetah Point.

'Madam, I come back in half hour after my breakfast,' the driver informed me.

I ordered an espresso and a cheeseburger. Though the espresso was more froth than coffee and the cheeseburger vegetarian, I enjoyed both. I paid my bill and took a walk around a well-kept garden full of flowers and large cages with geese, turkeys, parrots and a variety of water-fowl in them. I washed my face in the rest room and sat down on a chair in the lawn. The place seemed to be a popular stop.

Half an hour later we were back on the road. The countryside became uneven as hills appeared in the distance. There was less cultivation and more forests. Every now and then I saw trees ablaze with bright red flowers. I guessed this must be the flame of the forest. I must have dozed off. I woke up when the driver announced, 'Haridwar, Madam. Very holy city. *Har ki Paudi* is steps leading to Ganga Mata, holiest place in world.'

After we passed through a narrow, congested bazaar, I had short glimpses of the river. Then, a mountain wall on my left, a wide valley with the river flowing through it, and densely forested hills on the other side. We drove up and further up, along a winding dusty road, passed a lot of temples and sadhus smeared in ash and in ochre robes. Around 3 p.m. we turned off the main road, going down densely forested hillsides almost to the bank of the Ganga where there was a flat piece of land

paradise

growing vegetables and herbs and a broad white wall with a gate.

'Madam, Vaikunth Dhaam,' the driver announced triumphantly, and drove in.

It was exactly as it had appeared in the brochure—temple, courtyard, rooms. What the brochure had not captured were the lofty mountains all around, the path running down to the Ganga, the wind carrying the fragrance of pines and firs, the sound of the river rushing over rocks and boulders. I knew I was going to like this place.

I paid the driver, adding a hundred-rupee tip. He was pleased. More so because he got passengers to Haridwar and beyond. I went over to the reception counter.

'Yes, Madam,' said the man at the desk. 'You will be lady Margaret Bloom from New York. You wanted a room to yourself. It has been reserved for you for two months. The evening prayers start at six. Evening meal follows the prayers. I trust you have no alcohol or cigarettes with you—they're prohibited. I will show you to your room. Swamiji will receive you tomorrow, after the morning prayers.'

I was shown to my room. It had a charpai with

a mattress on it, a pillow and covers; a chair, a table, one light, one ceiling fan, two pictures on the wall—one of Lord Shiva with cobras around his neck and the Ganga pouring out of the dreadlocks piled up on his head, another of a bald man in saffron robes, who I presumed was Swamiji. There was no mirror. I learnt later that this was because Swamiji believed that looking at one's own face and admiring it boosted one's ego and vanity, both considered to be deadly sins.

'No loo? I mean, no bathroom?' I asked.

'Madam, they are outside, through that door,' the man said, pointing to a door in the western wall of the courtyard. 'Ladies and gents separately. Two European-style, the others Indian. Also washrooms if you wish to use soap or shampoo. They are not allowed in the Ganga.'

I shut the door behind him and stretched myself out on the charpai. It was not the most comfortable bed I had lain on, but it did not seem to matter. Though tired, I could get no sleep and kept wondering what I had got myself into. I heard people assembling for prayer. I heard them chant in unison and then sing something of which I only caught the last word, '*Harey*'. It was very soothing.

paradise

The singing stopped abruptly and I heard feet go pitter-patter along the verandah. I knew it was time for the evening meal. I mustered up courage and entered the dining hall. There were about a hundred men and women, including over a dozen Whites dressed in Indian clothes. I was given a warm welcome. 'Namastey,' I responded with a smile, and joined the palms of my hands.

A very small woman, she could not have been more than four-and-a-half feet tall, stood up and said, '*Behn*, you sit next to me.' I sat down on the bench beside her.

'My name is Putli, which means puppet. I am from Gujarat. And you?'

'My name is Margaret Bloom, I am from New York.' We shook hands; hers was the size of a three-year-old child's, and soft as silk.

Before the meal was served in brass plates there was a short prayer in Sanskrit chanted by a German disciple. A group of men and women went round the table serving spoonfuls of rice, daal and two dry vegetables, all dumped on the same plate. There were no spoons or forks. For the first time in my life I ate with my fingers. I was clumsy but assured myself I would learn fast. For dessert we had a *peda*. I did not touch the water in the glass placed before me. I had been warned against it. Putli noticed my hesitation and said, '*Ganga jal*, behn, water from the holy Ganga; it is clean and pure.'

I shook my head. 'I don't drink with my meals,' I lied.

We washed our hands and rinsed our mouths at basins at the end of the hall. Many men and women came and introduced themselves: Germans, Australians, Americans, English and Indians. Putli claimed me as her discovery. She took me by the hand when leading me to my room.

'You don't mind being alone? I am frightened of being alone at night. I sleep with other women in the dormitory,' she said.

'No,' I replied. 'I've always had a room to myself. I sleep much better.'

'Okay. I'll wake you up in the morning. We all go together to have a dip in the Ganga at sunrise. It is the routine of the ashram. Everyone follows it.'

I bade Putli goodnight and turned in. Despite the uncomfortable bed and hard-as-wood pillow, I had a sound, dreamless sleep. When I heard the ashram gong I thought I was still dreaming. Then there was a gentle knocking on the door and Putli

paradise

shouting, 'Margaret behn, it is time for *snaan*.'

I opened the door to let her in. 'What's *snaan*?' I asked.

'Holy dip. But first *sandaas*.'

'What's that?'

'You know, loo, toilet. You can also take a shower and soap yourself there. No soap is allowed in the river.' She had a small flashlight in one hand and a *lota* of water in the other. 'You take your toilet paper with you. And a towel. I will show you the way.'

It was still pitch dark. The sky was beginning to turn grey. Only the morning star shone brightly above us. I could see a few ghostly figures in the dimly lit courtyard going towards or coming back from the toilets outside. I tore a strip from the toilet roll I had brought with me, stuffed it in the pocket of my dressing gown and tossed a towel over my shoulder. I followed Putli's flashlight to the toilets. When I came out she was waiting for me, playing with the flashlight, making circles and squiggles with the beam in the dark. I followed her out of the ashram down a footpath leading to the river. The sky was lighter now. It was a gorgeous sight. Huge mountains, one which we were going down, and the other facing us. And in-between the broad expanse of grey-blue light, the river roaring its way over rocks and boulders towards the plains. I stopped for a while to take in the scene. I raised both my arms to the sky and shouted, 'This is paradise!'

'So it is,' said Putli. 'That is why it is called Vaikunth. Let's get over with the snaan before it gets too bright. There will be lots of men about. Some have dirty minds.'

Where the path ended the Ganga had split itself into two—the main stream on the other side and a shallower, slower-moving part on ours, divided by a largish island. There were some men a few yards upstream. Putli put down her flashlight, lota and towel on the ground and stepped into the water with her sari on. 'Ooo, it's cold. *Hari om, Hari om*. Come along, behn,' she urged.

I slipped off my dressing gown and stood stark naked for a while before quickly stepping into the water. It was icy cold. I rubbed my arms, thighs, belly and breasts before submerging myself neck-deep. I screamed, 'I'll freeze to death if I stay in here any longer,' and ran out to get my towel. Putli remained waist-deep in the river, filled the palms of her hands with water and offered it to the rising sun. After a while she came out shivering.

'Margaret behn, you have a nice body,' she said and cupped her little hands over my frozen breasts. 'How big and beautiful. Look at poor me.'

She slipped off her sari, took my hands and put them on her breasts. 'So small, like unripe mangoes.'

'Nothing wrong with them,' I told her, 'small but shapely. You'd better change into a dry sari or you'll catch a cold.'

We rubbed ourselves with our towels till our bodies were flushed red. It was exhilarating. She draped herself in a dry sari; I got into my dressing gown. I felt a little uneasy at the liberty Putli had taken with me. Almost immediately, I dismissed my fears—after all, she was still a child.

Back in the ashram we went to the temple. On the altar was a beautiful marble statue of Lord Shiva with the Ganga flowing out of his head. It glowed with a halo of coloured lights and was bathed in the fragrance of incense and fresh flowers. The temple filled with the tinkling of bells and soft chanting. It was mesmerizing. After the service we were put through half an hour of yoga asanas. It was sheer torture as I could not perform many of the postures.

The yoga teacher came over to me and said, 'Make haste slowly and you will succeed.' I didn't know what he meant. This was followed by half an hour of meditation. 'Empty your mind of all thoughts and concentrate on one point between your two eyes,' the teacher instructed. Much as I tried I could not empty my mind nor concentrate on one point. Once again I was assured that I would learn soon.

After meditation a man read out the division of duties for the day—who was to work in the kitchen garden, who was to cut vegetables, cook, serve food, wash the utensils. 'We will give Behen Margaret Bloom from America time to catch up with the duties we have to perform,' he said. I was asked to stand up so that I could be seen by everyone. Dutifully I joined the palms of my hands and said, 'Namastey. I am happy to be with you.' We had breakfast of pooris, sabzi and herbal tea. Thereafter we were left to do whatever we liked for the rest of the day till the *sandhya* prayer around sunset.

On the third day, the receptionist came and told me that Swamiji would like to see me after breakfast. Putli had mentioned that Swamiji sent for

paradise

the residents in turn, at least once a month, to ask them how they were doing. I went to his room as requested, touched his feet and sat down on the floor. Swamiji looked exactly as in the picture in my room. I was struck by the hypnotic quality of his eyes.

'You are Margaret Bloom from New York,' he said. 'I want to know why you came here and if you are getting what you expected to get.'

I told him everything—that I was fed up of the life I'd been leading, the excesses and indulgence. I told him my parents were divorced a long time ago and lived much the same way I did. 'It was all so pointless and without purpose. I was deeply disturbed, and decided to make a break. I looked for a place where I could find my true self. I came across Vaikunth Dhaam. From what I have seen in the last two days, I think I made the right choice.'

'Good, good,' he exclaimed, rubbing his hands. 'And how long do you expect to stay with us?'

'Till I am thoroughly cleansed of all the filth I have accumulated in my mind and body. Of course, if you allow me to stay till then. I will abide by your rules and pay for my keep for the time I am here. I can pay ten dollars a day. It is not very much, but that's all I can afford.'

'Anything you can afford is good enough; money is not important,' he said. 'If you have any problems, do not hesitate to come and see me. I am told Putli is looking after you. She is a very nice girl but she too has problems. You may be able to help her sort them out.'

I touched his feet and took my leave. No sooner had I got to my room than Putli came running in, very excited. 'So you met Swamiji! What did he ask you, and what did you say? Tell, tell.'

So I told her, and asked what had brought her to Vaikunth Dhaam.

'So many problems, problem after problem, behn. I was in my first year of college when my parents married me off to the son of a rich Gujarati merchant. I wasn't ready for marriage. All the fellow wanted was sex. He raped me the first night. Then again and again the second and third day. I hate sex. I hate men. I went back to my parents' house and told them that if they sent me back to him I would kill myself. They did not know what to do with me. They took me to doctors, psychiatrists, sadhus—anyone who could help. I did not want to have anything to do with any of them. Then I heard of this place and persuaded my parents to let me come here for a short time. They were glad to be rid of me. I have been here over three years. I don't ever want to go back. I want to live and die in Vaikunth Dhaam.' Putli was very worked up. She was close to breaking down. I stroked her head and asked her to take it easy. The exchange of confidences brought us closer to each other.

I realized that if I meant to stay in Vaikunth Dhaam for a while I would have to change my lifestyle a little. For starters, my American clothes made it difficult for me to do yoga asanas—try doing a headstand in a skirt! Also, bare legs attracted mosquitoes and flies. Some white women in the ashram wore saris, some dressed in salwar-kameez. I didn't care much for saris and decided the salwar-kameez would suit me better. I asked a German as tall as myself where she had got hers from. 'Right here!' she told me. 'Go a few yards up the road and you will come across a few shops that cater to the needs of our ashram and the villages around. You will find everything you want there.'

I asked Putli to come along with me. She said a firm no. 'Margaret behn, I've taken a vow never to step out of the ashram. When I go I'll be taken out feet first, on the shoulders of four men.'

There were things about Putli that made no sense to me.

I set off on my own. The shops stocked provisions of all kinds—from salt, pepper, spices, sugar and tea to joss sticks, *sindhoor* powder, candles, matchboxes and mosquito repellents. There were also bales of cloth, coarse silk and cottons. I noticed they had a few sets of readymade salwar-kameez outfits. I held a kameez against my chest to check whether it was my size and saw it was too small.

The shopkeeper came towards me. 'Okay, memsahib, I call *darzee*.' He called out to someone and a man appeared from behind the little store with a measuring tape and a pencil stuck behind his ear. He took my measurement down on a slip of paper. 'Choose cloth,' the shopkeeper said.

I picked a piece of saffron cotton that I thought would go best with my blonde hair. It was also the most popular colour among people tired of the world. I paid for four sets of clothes which the shopkeeper said would be delivered to me the next day. I also bought mosquito repellent lotion and joss sticks, some of which I wanted to give Putli.

Gradually I fell into the routine of ashram life.

paradise

I memorized some of the mantras they chanted. Putli taught me the Gayatri Mantra in praise of the sun, which she recited every morning when she took her dip in the Ganga. Slowly my joints began to ease up and I found that I had mastered the *padma asana*.

As the days grew warmer, I spent the afternoons taking a long siesta, lying naked in my room under a whirring ceiling fan. I persuaded Putli to take a second dip in the Ganga before sunset—that was the only place she was willing to go to outside the ashram. For Putli it was as though Vaikunth Dhaam was a mother's womb in which she found security, and the path to the Ganga the umbilical cord through which she drew sustenance. When I ventured beyond that path, I went alone. Once in a while I would take a bus to visit neighbouring towns—Lachhman Jhoola, Rishikesh, Haridwar—and take photographs, buy books and religious tracts. I understood very little of what I read but it didn't matter. After many years I was at peace with myself. I did not miss alcohol or smoking, and sex was the last thing on my mind.

After a month or so I felt I should see some more of the countryside and explore the towns that lay along the one and only road leading to the ashram. I joined a German couple interested in medicinal herbs and wildlife. We went deep into the surrounding forest. They picked up herbs and put them in their cloth bags. I spotted different kinds of deer, fresh droppings of elephants and even a couple of leopards disappear down the valley. The variety of bird life amazed me.

When I came back to the ashram and told Putli and the others what I had seen the only comment they made was, 'Really?' I discovered that Indians were not very interested in nature or wildlife.

The neighbouring towns and villages, I discovered, were quite nondescript, with a few shops around small temples. There were always ash-smeared sadhus about. Once I passed almost two dozen men, stark naked, as they strode along the dusty road with their penises dangling between their thighs. I asked the man sitting next to me in the bus who they were. 'Nagas,' he replied, 'naked sadhus.'

'That I can see,' I said, 'but why?'

He shook his head. 'Don't know.'

Indians weren't curious to know anything. Back in the ashram it was the German couple who told

paradise

me of the cult of Naga sadhus, and the trouble they created for the authorities when they assembled in large numbers at religious festivals. I wondered whether they got erections when they saw women but decided it was best to keep my curiosity to myself.

*

It got unbearably hot in June. Even in the high Himalayas it was difficult to walk in the sun. Occasionally a dust storm would blow; once we had a day and night of heavy rain and hail. Lightning flashed all night and the mountains echoed with thunder. Then it was over and the days were hot again. All day we heard the koels call. Then I heard the brain-fever bird, which I was told was the harbinger of the monsoon. Till the third week of June there was not a cloud in the sky. Putli and I spent a longer time in the river in the afternoons. The water was chilly and it was delicious lying in the shallows and letting it run over our bodies. Once a week I took my bottle of shampoo and a mug to the washrooms of the ashram. Putli would scrub my hair and wash the lather away with mugfuls of cold water, cooing all the while, 'Margaret behn, you have such lovely hair, made of gold thread. And look at mine, black and lifeless, hanging like a mouse's tail.'

'Don't be silly,' I would reprimand her. 'You have perfectly healthy hair.' I had realized by now that Putli needed constant reassurance.

It was one day in the last week of June that the German couple I had befriended asked me if I would like to go with them to Haridwar. They had hired a taxi that would pick them up after lunch and bring them back after they had seen the spectacular Ganga aarti at sunset. I jumped at the idea. I tried to persuade Putli to come along but she was quite firm in refusing my invitation.

'So I won't go to bathe in the Ganga this evening. I only go because of you,' she said with a long face.

'Can I get you something from Haridwar?' I asked, trying to get her out of her sulk.

'Anything you like,' she replied shrugging her shoulders.

It was to be a fateful day, momentous in a way I could not have anticipated.

When we left Vaikunth Dhaam it was hot and sultry. An hour or so after we reached Haridwar it

paradise

got worse. We left the taxi at the stand and told the driver we would be back as soon as the aarti was over. There, the German couple and I parted company. The couple had a camera and wanted to take pictures; I wanted to loiter along the bazaars. There was nothing I found worth buying for Putli. I settled for a dozen glass bangles of different colours and a head scarf with Rama printed all over it. Then I went to the ghats and headed towards Har ki Paudi where the main action was to take place.

I passed by many temples none of which was beautiful. I saw lots of well-fed cows, groups of sadhus and parties of pilgrims. At one secluded spot I saw four or five ash-smeared sadhus sitting around a smouldering fire smoking *chillums*. In the middle was a young man, the handsomest man I had seen, done up like Shiva. His hair was matted with a silver crescent moon stuck in it. He had nothing on him except a red jockstrap that covered his genitals. He sat ramrod straight, taking a puff of the chillum each time it was passed to him.

Our eyes met; his were large as a gazelle's. His gaze drew me towards him. It was as though I was hypnotized.

'Lady, come,' he said to me with a sinister

smile, and waved his acolytes away. I went and sat down beside him. He took a couple of puffs at his chillum and handed it to me. 'Try,' he commanded. I took the chillum from him, cupped my hands as he had done and inhaled the smoke. It was *ganja*, very much like the pot I had smoked back home. I hadn't touched the stuff for months, and it hit me hard. My head went into a swirl.

'Like it?' he asked. 'Give money to sadhu.'

I opened my purse and gave him a hundred-rupee note. He examined it against the light and then tucked it in his jockstrap. He kept gazing at me, my hair and my breasts, with the leering smile still stuck on his face. Then, very casually, he loosened his jockstrap and took out his erect penis. 'Like it?' he asked. 'Hundred rupee more, I put it in you.'

I knew I couldn't. I bent my head down in his lap and, kissing his penis, said firmly, 'No, not today. I'm going now.' I stood up, unsteady on my feet, and without looking back, headed towards Har ki Paudi.

Dark clouds had spread across the sky. A strong gale picked up. Just as I was approaching the sacred spot, a storm broke over my head. There was lightning and thunder, and it started to rain. I realized the aarti would be washed out and decided to head directly for the taxi stand and await my German friends. By the time I found the cab I was drenched to the skin and shivering with cold. Half an hour later the German couple arrived, also drenched, hugging their cameras under their shirts. 'Some rain!' said the man. 'We must get into dry clothes as soon as we can.'

It was pelting. I continued to shiver with cold through the car ride. On the way we passed a country liquor shop. I asked the driver to pull up. 'If I don't get a swig of whiskey or rum, I will get pneumonia,' I said to the Germans by way of explanation. The two of them said nothing. I bought myself a bottle of gin because it looked like water. I asked the vendor to scrape off the label. He dunked the bottle in a bucket of water beside him, then pulled it out and neatly peeled off the label. Evidently, he was used to doing this. I took a gulp and offered it to the Germans. 'No thank you,' they said, 'it is against the rules.' Rules be damned, I said to myself, I don't want to die of cold in a strange land. I felt better with the gin inside me and took a few more swigs as we went along.

It was after ten when we got to Vaikunth Dhaam. Everyone had turned in except Putli. She was waiting for me. 'Margaret behn, I nearly died of worry. Look at your clothes, they're dripping with water.'

I got into my room and stripped myself of the wet clothes. Putli rubbed me with the towel and helped me into my dressing gown.

'You must get into bed at once. I'll see if I can get you something to eat from the kitchen.' I shook my head. 'I don't want to eat anything. I just want the shivers to stop.'

'I am not going to let you sleep alone tonight. You may need help,' she said in a tone of authority.

A few minutes later she hauled in her charpai and bedding and arranged them along my bed. For a while she lay still, then stretched out her hand to feel my pulse.

'No fever, but you are still shivering. You chant *Om arogyam*, gone is my sickness, and you will feel better.'

I obeyed her. 'Om arogyam,' I repeated through my chattering teeth.

'I'll lie with you for a while and warm your body,' said Putli and slid into my bed and lay beside

paradise

me. I made room for her. I was still shivering and her warm body felt good, so I took her in my arms. She snuggled close, burying her face in my breasts. She began kissing them. I opened the front of my night gown so she could have direct access to my body. She kissed my breasts over and over again, first one then the other, suckling hungrily like a child. It was delicious. I was aroused. I kissed her on the lips, then kissed her all over her face. I took her tiny breasts in my mouth, one at a time. Putli was frantic with a demonic passion, clawing my arms, my shoulders, waist and buttocks. 'Margaret behn, lie over me. I want you. I love you.'

'My pet, you'll be crushed under my big body.'

'Crush me to pulp. Eat me,' she moaned. She lay there like a butterfly pinned to a board. I stretched myself out over her. She crossed her legs over my buttocks, dug her nails into them and pushed me against her. I don't know how long we went on. Our bodies were on fire, unquenchable. We thrashed against each other, rubbing our bodies, mauling each other like wild beasts, growling and moaning till we came. I was utterly exhausted. I thought little Putli would be half dead.

'You okay, my little one?' I asked.

'I'm fine. I'm with you, still lying in your bed,' she replied.

We lay next to each other. Sleep overcame me. I could barely feel Putli turning in my arms. A couple of hours later I sensed her kissing me all over my body. Starting from my toes she trailed her mouth along my legs, thighs, my cunt, belly and breasts.

'Kiss me on my lips again,' she pleaded. Half asleep, I complied. Soon we were going through the entire routine a second time. Only this time it took much longer. We lingered over our every move; it was done with more skill, and drained us of the little energy we had left.

We did not know when daylight came. It was still pouring, so the Ganga snaan was out of the question. We missed the morning prayer, the yoga asanas and the meditation. We also missed breakfast. More significantly, our absence was noted.

Apparently the German couple was worried about me, and told the others that I had been in poor shape the previous evening. Near lunchtime somebody knocked on my door and shouted, 'Margaret behen, are you okay? It is time for the midday meal.'

paradise

'I am fine,' I replied, shaking off my grogginess. 'I'll be out in a jiffy.' My body was stiff; I had nail marks on my neck, on my arms and down my back. Putli was tougher; she was more alert. But both of us looked badly ruffled up. We picked up our towels and clothes and ran to the bathrooms. We were back in a short while, ready to join the others for the midday meal.

I didn't say much besides admitting that I'd been drenched and had got the shivers. Putli was a torrent of explanation. 'Margaret behn had fever,' she said at the top of her voice. 'I felt her pulse. I gave her two Aspirins and pressed her body. She is not telling everything; I know she was in a bad way. Very, very bad. We hardly had any sleep; that is why we slept late.'

No one made any comment. Nobody believed her. What had happened the night before was written on our faces. And the residents of the ashram did not like what they read.

I knew it wouldn't be long before our conduct reached Swamiji's ears. He was known to be a strict disciplinarian who did not tolerate any breach of the ashram's rules. I was not sure how much he would be told but I was guilty on all counts: I had smoked ganja, kissed a man's penis, drunk half a bottle of gin and indulged in lesbian sex. He was not likely to accept any excuses and would almost certainly order me to leave Vaikunth Dhaam. My days in the earthly paradise were numbered. What would happen to Putli? She was fragile and had no one to turn to. She would be like a fish tossed out of water; she would wriggle helplessly for a while before she died.

We resumed our daily routine but the fun had gone out of it. Intermittent rains had made the path to the river very slippery. The Ganga was no longer a crystal clear and sparkling stream. The rains had washed a lot of mud into her. My heart no longer rejoiced to the chanting of prayer; I went through the yoga asanas mechanically and my meditation was disturbed by visions of the lecherous young sadhu, the liquor shop and the turbulent night with Putli.

It was a classic instance of a dog wanting to return to its vomit; a sow, having washed, wanting to wallow in the mire out of which she had come. I came to the conclusion that I deserved to be thrown out of Vaikunth Dhaam.

The day of reckoning was not long in coming.

paradise

One morning a few days later, the receptionist came to my room and told me that Swamiji would like to speak to me that afternoon at four sharp. I knew this was it. I reported at Swamiji's sanctum fully expecting the sentence of expulsion. I touched his feet and sat down on the floor beside his bed. He put his hand on my head and blessed me. 'Margaret *beti*, did you get what you were looking for in Vaikunth Dhaam?' he asked gently.

'I did, Swamiji. I have been very happy here. I know I have sinned and deserve to be punished.'

'Sin is a very strong word. Don't use it against yourself. What you have not finally decided on is the sort of life you want to lead. There is your Western way which most Indians are falling for, and there is our ancient way, puritanical you may say, which we in the ashram propagate. Yours is restless activity, rising higher and higher in whatever you do, earning more money, spending it so you can enjoy life—exotic food, wine, uninhibited sex. Striving hard just to have fun. You end up swallowing pills and lying on psychiatrists' couches. By the time you begin looking for peace of mind it is too late.

'Our way is diametrically opposite. Perform your duty to the best of your ability without considering the rewards. Do not envy other people's success. Look for joy—for *ananda*, not fun. Don't ruin your body with drinks, drugs and overeating. And above all, meditate on the purpose of life and it will give you peace of mind. The two ways, as I said, are diametrically opposite. You cannot combine them. You have to choose one or the other. You were fed up with the life you were leading and wanted to try out the spiritual path. You have done so for a few months but not been convinced of its truth. You found the longing to return to your older way of living too strong to resist.'

There was a long silence before I asked, 'You want me to leave the ashram?'

'I think it would be best for you.'

'What will happen to Putli? She has become very dependent on me.'

'That is another point in favour of your going away. Too much attachment to any person or thing always ends in suffering. You need not worry too much about Putli. She has nowhere to return to. I've taken her under my care for as long as I live. I will help her get over the attachment she has to you. It will take time, but she will, don't worry.'

'When do you want me to leave? I don't want Putli around when I do.'

paradise

'I have thought about that. There is no hurry—three days, four days, a week. Whenever you want to go. Don't tell Putli about our conversation. When you decide to leave I will ask her to be with me and tell her later that you have left.'

I held back the surge of emotion within me. I took out a hundred-dollar bill from my handbag and said, 'Swamiji, as a special favour please give this to Putli as a farewell gift.'

I left Swamiji with a heavy heart. Without telling anyone else I asked the receptionist to order a taxi to take me to Delhi in three days' time and to inform Swamiji about it. With Putli I was as cheerful as I could be. Her bed was removed from my room and we spent the remaining days together as if nothing had happened.

As planned, when my cab arrived, Putli was with Swamiji. I had only one valise in which I stuffed the few clothes I had and got into the car without saying goodbye to anyone. I wondered whether this was what Adam and Eve felt when they were thrown out of Paradise.

life's horoscope

Madan Mohan Pandey was by any reckoning a most unusual young man. 'So like his father in looks, so unlike him in everything else,' said people who knew the family. This was true. The father was never seen without his custom-made coat and trousers, even in the height of summer; the son had never been spotted in anything but dhoti-kurta and, since his youth, a saffron-and-gold *angavastra* around his neck. This was the most obvious contrast. There were other, deeper differences, apparent to those close to the family, and they had begun to surface when Madan Mohan was still a child.

Though both Madan Mohan's parents were Brahmins, they had discarded Brahmin practices and Westernized themselves. It was his father Hari Mohan Pandey's doing. He had made it to the

life's horoscope

Indian Civil Service the very first time he took the exam in Delhi, and thus found his way to England in the year 1928. In the one year of probation in Oxford, he had snipped off his topknot and discarded his sacred thread, the *janeu*. He had also committed the abominable crime of eating beef, and while in England, openly boasted to other Indian students, 'If you like to eat meat, there is nothing tastier than a juicy beefsteak. Try it with a glass of red vintage wine and you'll know what I mean.' He often quoted a Punjabi adage: 'Let it starve to death but do not kill it. Let vultures eat it but not mankind. Blessed be the Hindus, blessed their sacred cow.' Back home in India, however, he abjured eating beef. He explained: 'Here the cow is our mother, we drink its milk. We cannot kill and eat our *gau mata*. It is different in Europe. European cows are not sacred.' Everyone agreed that he was a clever, pragmatic young man who had a bright future as a bureaucrat of the Raj.

A young bachelor in the ICS was the most sought-after groom by parents of unmarried daughters. Hari Mohan had lost both his parents shortly after his return from Oxford, so the decision was entirely his own. He settled for Parvati Joshi, a convent-educated daughter of a Brahmin family who owned the largest department store in Delhi. She brought a huge dowry and was a docile girl willing to adapt herself to the European lifestyle of her husband, even when she wasn't entirely comfortable with it. Madan Mohan, their only child, was born a year after their marriage. Though the Pandeys had little faith in horoscopes, Parvati's father, Satyanand Joshi, had one cast for his grandson a few days after he was born. No one bothered to read it. Parvati simply rolled up the parchment, tied it up with a red ribbon and put it away in the safe in which she kept her jewellery.

By the time Madan Mohan started going to nursery school, it became evident that he had a mind of his own and was not going to be dictated to by his parents. His father insisted that everyone in the family speak in English because it was the language of the rulers and the future language of the world. Hindi or Hindustani was only meant to give orders to the servants or communicate with illiterate people. But little Madan Mohan persisted in speaking Hindi. His mother agreed and spoke in Hindi to him. His father refused to do so and hardly ever spoke to him. Madan Mohan's parents ate their meals with fork and knife; he wanted to eat with his fingers and threw a tantrum if he was not allowed to. Hari Mohan blamed his father-in-law, a pious and proud Brahmin, for his son's native ways, since the boy spent a lot of time with his grandfather who lived a short walk away on Curzon Road. Hari Mohan gave his servants strict instructions that *Chhotey Sahib* was not to be taken to Curzon Road, not even when their *Mataji* went over to meet her parents. But he could do nothing about Satyanand Joshi's visits to his own house when he was away on work, or in bed, two evenings a week, with the sisters Rasoolan and Akhtari of Chandni Chowk.

After nursery school, Madan Mohan was sent to the English-medium Modern School. But it was not English to which he paid much attention but Hindi, Sanskrit and mathematics. He did better in studies than his father. While his father's performance had been consistently above average through school, Madan Mohan excelled in every subject, including English. Hari Mohan was secretly proud of his son's scholarly achievements and was certain that if the boy sat for the Civil Services examination, he would make it without much difficulty. But he was not at all certain whether or not the boy would agree to sit for the exam. While still at school he had started talking of Gandhi in reverential tones, and had his school uniform made of the handspun khadi yarn that Gandhi was propagating.

After passing his matriculation, topping the Delhi list as everyone expected him to, instead of joining the prestigious St Stephen's College, Madan Mohan opted for Hindu College. 'I am a Hindu,' he told his father. 'I don't want to go to a Christian institution.' Being freed from wearing his school uniform of a blue shirt and dark blue shorts, he took to wearing white khadi kurtas and dhotis. And much to his father's irritation, he also began to sport a pigtail and a red *tilak* on his forehead. For his subjects, he chose Hindi, Sanskrit, philosophy and mathematics. He took an active part in intercollegiate debates. While other contestants spoke in English, Madan Mohan always spoke in Hindi, and his speeches were replete with quotations in Sanskrit from the Vedas, Upanishads and the Gita and anecdotes from the *Ramayana* and the *Mahabharata*. People began to call him Pandit Madan Mohan Pandey, or simply, Panditji. So under one roof, in a well-appointed bungalow of an ICS officer, lived three different people: Sahib, Mataji and Panditji.

life's horoscope

It was one day during his vacations, awaiting results of the BA exam, that Madan Mohan asked his mother if she still had the horoscope cast at his birth. 'Yes,' she replied, a little surprised and a little pleased too, for despite her husband's influence she remained a traditional Brahmin at heart. 'I'm sure it is still in my safe. Nobody has ever bothered to read it. Your father doesn't believe in such things, as you know.' His father didn't, Madan Mohan agreed, but he did, so could he see it, please. It was found as it had been put away over two decades ago, in a parchment scroll tied with a red ribbon. Madan Mohan took it to his room and opened it. On top it had the swastika emblem in saffron paste and the letter Om. Below this was a rectangle cut with different squares containing the names of eight planets. Madan Mohan had no difficulty in deciphering the contents of the horoscope, which were in Sanskrit. It read:

This child born in *samvat* 1989 of the Vikrami calendar corresponding to the date 15 August of the year 1931 of the Christian calendar will be most *honehaar* (gifted—this word was in Hindi). If properly nurtured by his parents, he will have a very bright future. He will be inclined to be somewhat headstrong, but if properly directed he will achieve great heights. If thwarted, he may turn into a rebel.

Madan Mohan paused. So far so good: every word of the horoscope had come true. His scholastic achievements did indeed presage a bright future. He had differences with his father. He was a rebel—with a cause. He continued to read:

He is likely to change his profession a few times. He may be in government service, an educationist and possibly even a politician. He is not likely to go into business. [*How could he? He was a Brahmin, not the son of a bania tradesman, muttered Madan Mohan.*] Whatever profession he undertakes, he will be highly successful. People born during the confluence of his planetary signs are leaders of men and are destined to achieve greatness. He may have a problem finding a suitable life partner and is advised to study the proposed bride's horoscope very carefully before giving his consent. If the horoscopes match, he should

life's horoscope

have a happy marriage and a large family of sons and daughters. His health may also create problems, as being somewhat intense he may suffer from stomach ulcers. He is advised to eat only sattvik food without garlic, asafoetida, onions, pickles, etc. He should abstain from liquor and tobacco. If he follows a strict regimen of food and does the prescribed yoga asanas he should live a long and healthy life.

Madan Mohan pondered over the contents of his horoscope before he rolled it up and re-tied it with the red ribbon. His mother entered the room and put a hand on his shoulder. '*Beta*, what does it say? We have never had it read. Your father never bothered with it.'

'*Theek hai*—it is okay. What it says about me has come true up till now. If Pitaji did bother to read it, he would realize that horoscopes are never false. Ma, do you know, in no other country in the world can people predict the future course of events as accurately as in India. It is a science known only to Indians. There are many other things in our *shastras* which prove that our forefathers also knew about electricity, aviation, telecommunications and much else that the Western world claims as its discoveries. The Westerners lie. We are pioneers in every field of science, mathematics, physics, chemistry, astronomy, astrology. You name it, we had it.'

Parvati had already come around to believing that her son was destined for a great future. He was not an eccentric, as her husband often described him. She gradually persuaded him that there was more to their son than he gave him credit for. 'Why can't he be like other young men of his age?' Hari Mohan grumbled. 'All this business of a long *chutia* dangling at the back of his head, tilak on his forehead, dhoti-kurta, spouting Sanskrit and whatnot! I agree he is a bright fellow, but why doesn't he move with the times?'

'Because he believes we Indians had a great past of which our generation knows very little. He wants to make us all aware of it,' Parvati said excitedly. 'He just told me what is written in his horoscope. It forecasts a great future for him. So far whatever it says has come true. If *Bhagwan* wills, the rest will also come true.'

'So be it,' mumbled Pandey Senior and fell silent.

*

life's horoscope

Madan Mohan topped the list in the university exam for the bachelor of arts degree, getting distinctions in Sanskrit and mathematics. He was immediately offered the post of lecturer in both subjects by the principal of Hindu College. He was only twenty at the time—the youngest ever to be offered a teaching job in the college.

His parents were delighted. But a teaching career had its limitations. He would undoubtedly become a professor, the head of his department, the principal of his college, and possibly even end up as the vice-chancellor of some university. But the civil services offered a much brighter future. His father pleaded with him—he no longer gave orders—to at least take a shot at the Indian Administrative Service. He could then decide his future career. The British had left, after all, and by joining the civil services now he would only be serving his own great country.

Madan Mohan gave in, only to please his father. He studied for the IAS exam. Apart from his favourite subjects, Hindi, Sanskrit and mathematics, he took Indian history. Studying for this paper confirmed his views of India's great Hindu past, the depredations caused by Muslim invaders and rulers and the brainwashing of Indians carried out during British rule. It made his blood boil.

He was third on the list of successful candidates. All the Central services would be his for the asking after the formality of a viva voce. Having gone so far to accommodate his father's wishes, he decided to put his foot down. He refused to go for the interview and so opted out of government service. He decided to accept the post of lecturer which was still open to him. The number of parents of nubile daughters who had approached the Pandeys for a marriage alliance when Madan Mohan cleared the written exam for the IAS, dropped sharply. When his mother told him about it, Madan Mohan scoffed: 'See how low our society has fallen? Everyone is up for sale. I will put a stop to all this nonsense.'

Despite their disappointment at Madan Mohan refusing to join any civil service, his parents had reason to admire him. How many young men in the country would have the guts to walk away from a prestigious job and accept a lowly-paid lecturer's salary? Their wide circle of relatives and friends, though they would no longer give their daughters in marriage to their son, showered praise on him. 'If India had more of his kind of young men,' they said, 'we would have a different story to tell.' And so

life's horoscope

Madan Mohan embarked on a career as an educationist, filled with a great sense of purpose. He would rescue young minds from false histories. On his first day as lecturer, he wore a new khadi kurta-pyjama, a longer than usual tilak on his broad forehead, and, for the first time, a silk angavastra around his neck, saffron with a gold border.

It is ironic that although Madan Mohan had chosen the teaching profession and mastered the subjects he taught, his students did not take to him. He was too pedantic, too rigid in his views, and did not like being questioned. According to him, now that British rule in India was over, it was time Hindus regained their cultural and scientific inheritance, and for this it was necessary to suppress the Muslims or throw them out of the country. Hindus would revive ancient Hindu science and technology enshrined in the vedas. The ancients knew all about aviation long before the Wright brothers flew a plane. Didn't Shri Ram, Sita, Lakshman and Hanuman fly from Sri Lanka to Ayodhya in the Pushpak Viman? Didn't Hanuman parachute down from the aircraft to land ahead of the rest of the party and alert the people of Ayodhya so they could give their beloved Ram a fitting welcome? Madan Mohan talked of Ayurveda as the greatest system of medicine and Vaastu as the foundation of all architecture. He mocked Muslim claims to having built the Qutab Minar and the Taj Mahal: 'They were not builders; they were destroyers of great temples built by Hindu architects,' he said. 'You read ancient Sanskrit texts and they will open your eyes. Don't accept what is written in English textbooks as gospel truth; they belittle everything our ancestors did only to glorify their own tiny achievements.' And he went on in this manner while most of his students struggled to stay awake.

Attendance in Madan Mohan's classes began to drop as students opted for other subjects after their mid-term exams. Boys and girls began referring to him in derision as Mahamahopadhya Chutiadhari (wearer of the pigtail) Pandit Madan Mohanji. Some invented new names for his initials: MM—*Maha Moorakh*, the great fool. Reports reached the Principal's ears that Pandey, despite his brilliance, was not a good teacher. By the end of the year, Madan Mohan sensed that neither students nor the teaching fraternity were ready to accept his revolutionary ideas. He was not the one to make

life's horoscope

compromises. If they didn't want him, he did not want them. And that was that.

The college authorities sensed that if they fired Madan Mohan there would be an uproar in university circles; if he resigned it would bring a bad name to the college. It was Madan Mohan himself who found a way out of the predicament. He applied for long leave without pay. With a great show of regeret the principal accepted his application and assured him that the post of lecturer he had held would not be filled till he decided to return.

Madan Mohan's parents began to despair of their son all over again. 'God gives with one hand and takes away with the other,' remarked his father. 'God gave him brains and God also made him wayward.'

'He needs a stabilizing influence in his life,' Parvati ventured. 'Perhaps a good, understanding wife will make him more responsible.'

'We had dozens of the richest Brahmin families offering their daughters to us. Who will want to hand over his child to an unemployed college teacher?'

'What do you mean by unemployed teacher?' Parvati retorted angrily. 'He is an outstanding scholar, the likes of which this country does not have!'

Pandey Senior had no response to that but to throw up his hands in despair and grunt. After a while he said, 'You have to ask him if he's willing to get married. If I know him he will say no and give you a long lecture on the merits of remaining a *brahmachari*, with quotations on celibacy from Sanskrit texts that only he understands.'

His wife glowered at him. She did not like anything sarcastic being said about her son. But she knew that it would not be easy to get round the boy—he was unpredictable.

Unpredictable he proved to be. Parvati broached the subject as tactfully as she could. 'Beta, you are getting on twenty-four now. Isn't it time you found a life companion to look after you? We are getting old and find it increasingly difficult to look after ourselves. Your father has asthma. I have arthritis in my knees and struggle to walk. We need someone to run the house.'

Madan Mohan did not scoff at the idea as she had feared he would. Instead he asked, 'Has any family approached you?'

'Many families have made enquiries,' she began

life's horoscope

happily. 'We put them off by saying you didn't have a *pukka* job and were not ready for marriage. Of course, you don't need a job if you don't want one. You have this house; it is yours after we go. And there is enough money in the bank to last your lifetime. Both of us are eager to see you married. It is for you to decide.'

Madan Mohan pondered over the matter for a while, then replied, 'If that is what you want, I will abide by your wishes.'

His mother beamed a radiant smile and put her right hand on his head. '*Jeetey raho, beta*! May you live long. Would you like to see the girls whose parents have approached us, or their photos?'

'No, Ma. I don't want to see them or their photos. You choose. But I would like to examine the horoscopes of the girls you shortlist. I am in no hurry.'

Having left his teaching job, Madan Mohan joined the Hindu Sangathan. He had heard favourable accounts of the organization. It aimed to re-educate Hindus about their glorious past, the havoc caused by Muslim invaders and the insidious anti-Hindu propaganda carried out by Christian missionaries under British patronage. Its members assembled every morning in different parks of the city, dressed in white shirts, baggy khaki shorts and black caps. They were mainly shopkeepers with paunches and spindly, hairy legs. They were put through a drill with lathis, and performed yoga asanas and wrestled clumsily in the mud like overgrown schoolboys. The sessions ended with short sermons delivered by their leaders. Madan Mohan joined the *shakha*, or branch, closest to his home. His reputation as an extraordinary scholar and a champion of Hindu pride had preceded him. He was given a warm welcome. He was asked to deliver the morning sermons and was invited by other shakhas in the city to speak to them. Soon the chief of the Delhi Sangathan invited him to the central office. He was welcomed with a cordial embrace. The chief was a thin elderly man with thick glasses and a Charlie Chaplin moustache. He spoke very slowly. 'I have heard great praise of your dedication to the Sangathan and the way you expound its ideals. You have qualities of leadership. I have also made enquiries about your background. You come from a noble and distinguished Brahmin family. You have been a professor and believe in the ideals of *brahmacharya*. Isn't that so?'

life's horoscope

Madan Mohan replied candidly, 'I thank you for your kind words. I was a lecturer and not a professor. I am single but plan to get married soon.'

The old chief looked disappointed. 'Some of our leaders remained celibate all their lives because they wanted to devote all their time and energy to the Sangathan.'

'I intend to devote myself entirely to the Sangathan, but I have to get married; I have given my word to my mother. I am her only child.'

The chief was impressed. 'That is very noble of you. A mother is goddess incarnate, her wishes should be treated as commands. Several of our leaders are also *grihasthis*. But being a householder does not mean that you are any less committed to the cause. What really counts is dedication.'

'You can count on me for that,' replied Madan Mohan, and then the thin man in khaki shorts embraced him again.

*

It did not take long for Madan Mohan's mother to revive proposals they had received earlier—all from Brahmin families. As required, all of them furnished horoscopes, quite a few sent their daughters' biodatas and photographs as well. Hari Mohan and Parvati examined the proposals first and weeded out those they considered unsuitable. They were left with a dozen which they put before their son. 'I don't want to see any photographs,' he said firmly. 'I would like to know the exact time and place of their birth so I can make my calculations and check if their horoscopes have been properly cast. It is common for parents of girls to lie about their age. I will also examine their biodatas. I expect my wife to be educated.'

'We've seen to that,' replied his father. 'We rejected those who have not been to college. All these girls are graduates in something or the other: English, history, Hindi, home science. It is now for you to decide.'

Madan Mohan took the horoscopes to his room and spread them out on the work table. From his study of the subject he had concluded that the best match for a Leo—he was a Leo—was a Taurus. Only three applicants in the lot were born under the sign. He scanned their biodatas. Two had been educated in Indian *paathshalas*, one was from a convent and had taken her BA degree in English literature from St John's College, Agra—a Christian

life's horoscope

missionary college—on a scholarship. Madan Mohan thought over it. Though he set no store by knowledge of English literature, he felt that his future wife should have a good command over the language, as most books in his personal library were in English. It was also a useful asset when meeting foreigners and people who could not speak Hindi. The Christian missionary education bothered him, but he was quite certain that like many Indians of her class the girl had not really thought about the pernicious influence of the proselytizing Christians. She needed to be educated, to have her eyes opened to the truth, and he was confident he could do that. He took a second and a third look at the girl's biodata and horoscope. She was one of the many daughters of a school teacher in Mathura. She was five years younger than him: that was ideal. Her name was Mohini Joshi.

'Find out what you can about this girl Mohini Joshi,' he told his parents. They were overjoyed. 'Joshis are of the same class of Brahmins as us Pandeys,' said his mother. 'Pandey-Joshi alliances are common. Her father appears to be a man of modest means, which is better. One should not make an alliance with a family above one's own.'

So Pandey Senior wrote to Joshi Senior and invited him and his wife over to Delhi. A few days later the Joshis arrived at the Pandeys' doorstep with their daughter. They were awed at the size of the bungalow and its lavishly furnished interior. They joined the palms of their hands as if in prayer and said, 'We are humble people who have very little to give in the way of dowry, except our daughter.' Mohini went down on her knees and touched the feet of the Pandeys. Both put their hands on her head and blessed her. 'We are not looking for a dowry,' said Parvati Pandey. 'Bhagwan has given us plenty. All we want is a nice girl for our only child. He, as you know, is one in a million. He refused to join government service after being selected for it and went into the teaching profession. Now he is a full-time social worker dedicated to the service of his country.'

Tea was ordered. Parvati asked the servant to inform Chhotey Sahib that the Joshis had arrived. Madan Mohan came down from his room, dutifully touched the Joshis' feet and allowed Mohini to touch his. Parvati poured out the tea, asked the Joshis by turn how much sugar they liked, and had the bearer hand them their cups. She and her

life's horoscope

husband were appalled to see all three pour the tea into their saucers and slurp noisily as they sipped it. Madan Mohan was charmed: where could you meet Indians these days who drank tea out of saucers?

There were long pauses of silence. Parvati did her best to keep the conversation going. Her husband wasn't sure whether he should speak to them in Hindi or English. Mrs Joshi evidently didn't speak the language and her daughter sat dumbly looking down at her feet. Madan Mohan was not much help either. He kept staring at Mohini, looking her up and down. She was certainly fair, he noted—as most Brahmins undefiled by non-Hindu blood were. She was short and petite and had long, glossy, heavily oiled hair tied up in a big bun behind her head. Her bosom was beautifully rounded, snugly ensconced in her full-sleeved blouse, and when she touched his feet, he had noticed that she had the kind of hips described in one Hindu text as 'auspicious, child-bearing hips'. She had painted her toe nails red and wore a thin silver anklet on one foot. Mohini sensed she was being assessed and kept her head bowed. Then the impulse to see the young man who might become her husband overcame her shyness and she looked up. She thought he looked exactly like a young Brahmin rishi, one who had just had his morning dip in the icy waters of the Ganga. He looked clean and in robust health. She was pleased at the prospect of being his wife. Their eyes met for a brief moment. Her face lit up with a winsome smile. He was bowled over.

While Hari Mohan occupied himself drinking a second cup of tea that he did not want, his wife and their son whispered into each other's ears. Then Parvati fished out a small box of blue velvet from her handbag and handed it to Madan Mohan. He drew up a chair next to Mohini and sat down beside her. He took her left hand in his and slipped a gold ring with a diamond on her third finger. Mohini was overcome with embarrassment and could think of nothing else but to go down on the carpet and place her head between his feet like a puppy.

The Joshis were overwhelmed with gratitude. 'For our Mohini fate has opened the gates to heaven in all its refulgent glory,' said the father. He said this in chaste Hindi, prompting Hari Mohan to say '*Bas, bas,*' irritably to stop the man before he launched into Sanskrit shlokas. The mother added, addressing Parvati, '*Behenji*, we are poor people, we have very little to give you except our daughter.

life's horoscope

From now on she is your property. You are her mother.'

Hari Mohan interrupted gruffly, 'I told you we don't want anything in the way of a dowry. We don't believe in big *baraats*, no band *baaja*. It will be a simple wedding according to vedic rites as my son wishes, with the minimum of guests. I think it will be best if you come to Delhi with your immediate family. I will reserve a *baraat ghar* for you—there is one not far from here. You can stay there and have the *havan* in the garden. We will fix the day of the marriage after our son has consulted his star charts. He claims to know more about auspicious days than any astrologer.'

The Joshis fell at the feet of the Pandeys. 'We are mere bricks of a sewer and our daughter will adorn the top floor of a palace! Bhagwan has answered our prayers,' said Mr Joshi with tears in his eyes. The Joshis embraced the Pandeys many times before they got onto the three-wheeler phut-phut on which they had come, to return to the inter-state bus terminal and take the bus to Mathura.

*

The Pandeys were pleasantly surprised that their son had so readily agreed to get married. They were confused; they had to admit that they did not really know how his mind worked. For Madan Mohan it was quite straightforward: he always went by the sacred texts. A man's lifespan was a hundred years, divided into four equal parts. The first quarter, brahmacharya, was for study, and during this time he had to remain celibate. Madan Mohan was twenty-four and still a virgin. He was now about to enter into grihastha—the life of a householder: acquire a wife, have children, and earn his livelihood. For this, too, there were rules, and he was following them diligently. The *Kamasutra* prescribed that a man should marry a woman at least three years younger than himself: Mohini was five years his junior. The *Kamasutra* divided men and women into three categories depending on the sizes of their genitals, and indicated which category of women made ideal wives. From the little he had seen of her, Mohini was almost certainly a *mrigini*, a doe—petite, slim and coy; clearly a suitable bride. She certainly could not be a mare. Nor a *hasthini*—a she-elephant—a woman with a large vulva and an enormous appetite for sex.

He was not entirely sure about his own category: was he a hare, a bull or a horse? He did not like to

life's horoscope

think of himself as a hare—they were as randy as rabbits and had small penises. He had never measured his organ but its size impressed him. He could be a bull or a horse. Yes, that was most likely—though that might create problems for the petite Mohini; he would have to be gentle with her. He would adjust to her, and give her time to adjust to him, by controlling his lust like a yogi.

*

Madan Mohan was particular about dates. It was late in March that the Joshis had come over with their daughter and he had agreed to marry her. Since then Joshi had written twice to his father enquiring about his health and indicating that he did not believe in long engagements; as soon as their son-in-law-to-be had decided on an auspicious day, the Joshis would like to hand over their daughter to his family. He wrote a letter to Madan Mohan, too, with the same request. Mohini had also written two letters to Madan Mohan, both in English and in block letters, addressing him as 'MY ONE AND ONLY MADANJI' and telling him how much she was looking forward to becoming his 'LOVING AND FAITHFUL WIFE'. She signed off as 'YOUR BELOVED MOHINI'. Madan

Mohan replied to their letters in a business-like tone, telling Mohini's father that they would soon be hearing from him about a suitable date, and assuring Mohini of his affection and advising her to acquaint herself with sacred Hindu texts on marriage.

The 15th of August was Madan Mohan's birthday. He would turn twenty-five, and could then end his brahmacharya and enter *grihastha*. The marriage ceremony could take place on any day after that. But by that time the monsoons would have set in. The gods would retire under the ocean. It was not auspicious to have marriages during the rainy season. Sometime late October or early November would be more suitable. For a more precise time, he would need to study carefully the books he had collected on astrology.

Madan Mohan had recently begun using B.V. Raman's *Hindu Predictable Astrology* as a textbook on the subject. It was heavily marked and underlined on several pages. To him, Raman was a genius, and his book, based on ancient Sanskrit texts, was far more reliable than the works of Nostradamus and other Europeans who were mere magicians—and bad ones, too, since magic had been perfected in India, not in the West. He also subscribed to *The*

life's horoscope

Astrological Magazine, published from Bangalore, and *Babaji*, edited by Lachhman Das Madan of Delhi. Every new book and magazine he read on astrology confirmed his opinion that the wise sages of India's glorious past were geniuses. They had divided not only the months of the year but also the hours of the day and night into periods that were auspicious and those that were unlucky: Rahu Kaal, Yamagand, Gulika Kaal. With these principles to guide him, Madan Mohan consulted his own and Mohini's horoscopes. He decided that the 31st of October would be the most suitable day for their marriage and 9.30 p.m. the most suitable time for the nuptial ceremony. Hari Mohan Pandey wrote to Mohini's father informing him of this.

In the meantime, Madan Mohan read and re-read the *Kamasutra*. He marvelled at the precision with which the sage Vatsyayana had analysed sexual differences between men and women and given detailed advice on how they could get the best out of each other. He knew about the three classifications of the two genders depending on the sizes of their genitals. He had recently measured his penis at rest and when erect with a measuring tape and it had confirmed his opinion that he was either a bull or a horse, probably the latter. But how did one plumb the depths of a woman's vagina? He came to the conclusion that in Vatsyayana's time Hindu scientists must have invented some kind of dipstick for the purpose, of the kind used to gauge the amount of oil in a car. They had made all the necessary calculations centuries ago, so that now people like him could study the scriptures and tell, just by looking carefully at a woman, the size of her vagina.

He read with amazement about the *chatushashti*—sixty-four—different postures that couples could adopt during intercourse. And about the sexually sensitive points in a woman's body— where and how to kiss her, bite her, dig his nails in her—and the kinds of noises she would make in the heat of passion. Vatsyayana was meticulous in his research and quoted other authorities on sex where they differed with him. He was a true scholar and a sage, and Madan Mohan was full of admiration for him.

However, he was dismayed to read Vatsyayana's advice that a man should not be in a hurry to consummate his marriage on the first night but wait at least three days to win over his bride's confidence and only enter her when she was fully aroused and

life's horoscope

eager for the union. He pondered over the problem. He got some books from the Nehru Library to see if they had anything on the subject of deferring sexual intercourse after marriage. He was delighted to find yet another piece of evidence of the West borrowing ideas from ancient Hindu texts. As usual, the Germans had been the first to pick up Oriental wisdom. In several parts of that Aryan country it was a practice not to allow a newly-wed couple access to each other for a few days. In Swabia, three days' abstinence was prescribed—the same as in the *Kamasutra*. They were known as Tobias nights. Convinced, all over again, of the greatness of Hindu thought and practice, Madan Mohan decided that if he could remain celibate for twenty-five years, he could remain celibate for twenty-five years and three days.

*

Madan Mohan took charge of his wedding arrangements. He went to the baraat ghar in Kaka Nagar, inspected the rooms and furniture and gave instructions on how many coloured lights were to be put up on the parapets of the building and in the trees in the garden; where the havan pit was to be dug and where the three-man team of shehnai players was to be seated. He chartered a bus to pick up the Joshis, their relatives and friends early on 30th October, get them to Delhi by noon and then take them back to Mathura, minus Mohini, the next afternoon. He informed his prospective father-in-law of the arrangements, telling him that the bus could carry no more than fifty passengers and advising him to bring their family priest with them. The only tasks he left for his parents were to buy gifts for Mohini's family and arrange a lunch reception in their house on the day following the wedding.

Through all this he also continued attending and addressing shakha meetings, doing his yoga asanas and studying the *Kamasutra*. Starting a week before his wedding date he got a masseur, trained in the science of Ayurveda, to give him an oil massage every morning. He followed the massage with a hot bath, scrubbing his body with a loofah to rinse out the oil. It invigorated his system and left a mild fragrance of herbal oil on his body.

Things went exactly according to schedule. The Joshis arrived in Delhi on time. With them they brought their own pandit, and the little dowry they could afford to give their daughter: a sewing machine, a small fridge, six sarees and some jewellery. The Pandeys invited their closest relatives and friends, who were to form their son's baraat, for tea on the afternoon of the 31st of October. By the time the tea party was over, the sun had set and the guests were instructed to have their cars lined up behind the larger of the Pandeys' two cars which had been decked up with strings of jasmine flowers. Madan Mohan had put his foot down on riding on a horse led by a brass band. He did not wish to make a spectacle of himself. He rode in the car with his parents to the baraat ghar. By the time they arrived, the coloured lights had been switched on and the shehnai players had struck up their plaintive whine. The Joshis welcomed the Pandeys and their party. Mohini was gently pushed in front, half her face covered by her sari *pallu*. She put a garland of jasmines around Madan's neck; in return Madan put a garland around hers. The guests were conducted to the lawn to partake of a vegetarian feast of pooris, *kachauris*, sweets and soft drinks.

While the guests were still guzzling food and drinks, Madan was taken indoors for a session of banter with Mohini's sisters and girl cousins. They seated him in their midst and placed a platter of sweets and a tumbler of sharbat before him. '*Doolhaji*, sample some of our home-made *halva* and sharbat,' they chorused. Madan was too smart for them. 'You taste some first, then I'll take it,' he said. It turned out that the sweets were full of chillies, the sharbat full of salt. Disappointed that their prank had failed, the girls removed the platter. Even as they did so, one girl came up behind Madan Mohan, pulled his chutia and asked, 'Other animals have tails on their bums, why do you have one on your head?' Madan Mohan turned around sharply, grabbed the girl's pigtail and brought her down to her knees. 'You touch my chutia again and I'll make sure you don't have a single hair left on your head!' he said angrily. 'Learn to respect your traditions!' Mohini's mother, who was at the door, rushed in and intervened, 'Bas, stop this nonsense. Don't trouble your *jeejaji*. It is time for the *pheras*.'

The havan pit was lit and pandits of both families took their places beside it. The auspicious hour for solemnizing the marriage was at hand. Madan Mohan and Mohini were seated side by side. The pandits began to chant marriage hymns from the Vedas, feeding the sacred fire with spoonfuls of ghee and

life's horoscope

instructing the bride and bridegroom to toss sacred offerings into it. Madan Mohan, of course, needed no instructions since he was familiar with all the hymns and rituals. This went on for nearly half an hour. Then the couple was asked to stand up. One end of Mohini's saree was tied to a pink scarf that Madan Mohan wore around his neck, and as they went round the sacred fire seven times, family members and friends gathered around and showered rose petals on them. Madan Mohan put a black-beaded *mangalsutra* around Mohini's neck, applied *sindhoor* in the parting of her hair, and the two were pronounced man and wife.

It was a custom in the Joshi clan that the bridegroom spent the first night in the bride's home, all by himself. It was only after he had taken his bride to his own home that he was allowed to consummate his marriage. Since the Joshis had no home of their own or even relatives in Delhi, they prepared a room in the baraat ghar for their son-in-law. Madan slept fitfully. The small room had bare white walls and only a couple of chairs, and the bed was an uncomfortable string charpai with pillows as hard as wood. Despite the spartan routine of yoga asanas and the Sangathan drill, Madan Mohan found this trying since he was used to sleeping on a soft bed with feathered pillows. Then there were thoughts about entering the second stage of his life. He was no longer a brahmachari but a man with a wife to look after, whose needs he had to cater to and whom he had to take out with him wherever he went. He would have to make a lot of adjustments in his daily routine. But there would be compensations, of course—a woman to make love to whenever he wanted, a woman to look after his needs as his mother had done, and bear his children. Most of all he looked forward to the next three days, during which he would prepare Mohini to yield herself to him. The *Kamasutra* advised grooms to be patient and gentle with their virgin wives. If she was put off by her first experience of sex, it would take the poor girl months or years to come to terms with it. It was well past midnight by the time Madan Mohan finally fell asleep. He was still groggy the next morning when, to the sad notes of the shehnai, Mohini bid a tearful farewell to her family and was driven away in the Pandeys' car to her new home.

There was a stream of visitors all morning till late into the evening at the Pandey residence; relays

life's horoscope

of bearers serving tea, coffee, cold drinks and snacks. By the time the last visitor left, and blessings sufficient for several lifetimes had been bestowed on the newly-wed couple, it was time for dinner. No one had appetite for more food and everyone was exhausted—most of all Mohini. The family sat around the table sipping tomato soup, which was all they could take. Parvati escorted the bridal couple to their bedroom, blessed them and retired. Madan Mohan bolted his bedroom door from the inside and sat down on the sofa.

'You must be very tired,' he said to Mohini. 'Come and sit beside me so I can have a good look at you. And you tell me all about yourself.' To his surprise, Mohini, who had looked ready to collapse with exhaustion only a few minutes before, sprang back to life, pulled the pallu from her head, grabbed his hand and said boldly, 'Take a good look. Do you like what you see?'

This was not at all according to the holy book on sex. Perhaps she had not read it. 'Yes, you are a very good-looking young lady,' Madan Mohan replied, 'a classic example of a mrigini.'

'A what?'

'Mrigini—a doe. According to the *Kamasutra*

there are three types of women: a deer-woman, a mare-woman and an elephant-woman, depending on the sizes of their private parts. You are small and well-formed; you have to be a mrigini. Didn't you read the *Kamasutra*? I'd asked you to read the sacred Hindu texts on marriage.'

'*Harey Ram*! What kind of a family do you think I come from! My parents never allowed dirty books in the house.'

'It is not a dirty book,' said Madan Mohan sternly. 'It is the oldest classic in the world on marriage and the art of love.'

'I don't know about such things. But I would have you know that when I was in college, they had a beauty contest. I was unanimously voted beauty queen of the year.'

'You entered a beauty contest?' he asked rather alarmed. '*Chheeh! Chheeh!* They are Western practices, very unbecoming for Hindu women. How did your parents allow you to do something so vulgar?'

Mohini was crushed. 'I did not tell my Ma and Pitaji about it till after I was crowned. They did not like my exposing myself and allowing my breasts, waist and buttocks to be measured, but they were

life's horoscope

quite pleased with the outcome. I have a good figure. My friends in college told me I have the same measurments as that Swedish girl who became Miss Universe last year. Only, I am short, just five feet two inches.'

'That is an appropriate height. I am five feet seven; a woman should be suitably shorter than her husband,' Madan Mohan said stiffly and then fell silent.

'You are not *gussa* with me, are you?' Mohini pouted.

'No, I am not angry. What is past is past. But no more beauty contests. They are very un-Hindu,' he replied firmly.

'Thank God!' Mohini sighed dramatically in relief, with one hand on her chest. With her other hand, she still clutched his. He was the husband, he was meant to take the lead, but it was *she* who was calling the shots. This confused Madan Mohan. There were a few moments of awkward silence before he remembered the next step he had to take. He fished out a betel leaf from his silver *paan daan* and said, 'Here, I have a special paan for you.' He held it to her lips. 'You must take half of it from me,' she said and took half the paan in her mouth, the other half sticking out of her teeth. She put a hand on his thigh and leant towards him. Madan Mohan was amazed by her brassiness. As he bit into the half sticking out of her mouth, she flung her arms around his neck and gave him a full-blooded kiss on his lips.

This was outrageous! She was flouting all the sacred rules. Despite her petiteness she was perhaps not a mrigini after all!

'Are you by any chance a hasthini, young lady?' he asked weakly.

'A what? Do I look like an elephant to you?' she demanded angrily.

'No, no, it has nothing to do with the size of your body,' he explained apologetically, 'but . . . but—'

'What but-but? First a mrigini, then a hasthini— I am an innocent little girl, I don't understand all this.'

'That is because you have never read the *Kamasutra*.'

'I told you Pitaji would not allow such books in our home.'

'Pity! It would have taught you something about the art of making love.'

life's horoscope

'Professor sahib, you don't have to read books to learn how to make love. We are married. I make love to you, you make love to me. Isn't that simple?'

'No, it is not so simple,' he replied. 'Do you know there are sixty-four ways of making love?'

'Sixty-four!' she exclaimed with wide-eyed wonder. 'I thought there was only one. You teach me all sixty-four. I promise to be a good disciple.' She gave him another kiss on his lips. 'But we can't spend our first night of marriage as if we are in a classroom. That is not the meaning of *suhaag raat*.'

'No, it is not,' he said pulling her away from him. 'The first night should be spent in getting to know each other. You tell me about yourself and I will tell you about myself. On the second night we do the same but go a little further in disclosing more intimate details. Hindu authorities on the subject advise that love-making should start after the third night.'

'*Uffo*!' she exploded. 'What a strange man you are! If we are to do nothing on our suhaag raat, we may as well go to sleep. What is this nonsense about talking! I am very tired.' She got up from the couch and walked briskly to the bathroom. She rinsed her mouth, washed her face and went straight to the bed prepared for them. She brushed away the rose petals strewn on the sheets and lay down in her wedding sari with her face turned towards the wall. Madan Mohan sensed she was sulking; she was evidently a bad-tempered girl and would have to be handled very carefully. He would be patient.

He went to the bathroom, brushed his teeth and took a shower, carefully soaping his armpits and groin. He changed into a fresh pair of kurta-pyjamas and sat on the nuptial bed. After a while he put his hand on Mohini's shoulder and asked, 'Are you gussa with me?'

She shrugged her shoulder and growled, 'Don't touch me till you get permission from your holy dictionary. I don't want to talk to you.'

Madan Mohan resigned himself to a sleepless night. For a long while he lay on his back, staring at the ceiling. Then he switched off the bed light and shut his eyes. Mohini lay facing the other way, stiff as a log. The *Kamasutra* had nothing to say about sulking brides. Slowly sleep overcame him.

Mohini was up before him. She squeezed toothpaste onto her forefinger and rubbed her gums vigorously. She did not know how to operate the

life's horoscope

shower, so she filled the steel bucket from the tap and since there was no *lota*, used the enamel mug placed on the cistern of the WC to wash herself. She changed into a new silk sari and without saying a word to her husband went down to join his parents. Hari Mohan Pandey was reading the morning papers; his mother was in the puja room. Mohini touched her father-in-law's feet, received his blessings and joined her mother-in-law.

They heard Madan Mohan come down and join his father for tea. Parvati quickly finished her part of the ritual and told her daughter-in-law, '*Bahu*, I will send my son to join you. My puja is short and basic, but he is very particular about the rituals he follows. You must pray together and learn from him. I will help the servants prepare breakfast.' She went out and informed her son, 'Mohini is waiting for you to perform puja. She does not know the rituals we follow. I will have the breakfast laid out.'

As soon as Madan had gone into the puja room, his mother walked up to the bridal chamber. She saw the rose and jasmine petals she had strewn on the bed the evening before scattered on the floor. That was a good sign: the couple had slept together. She examined the bed sheet: there were no tell-tale stains of blood or seminal discharge. They had probably not consummated their union. Her son was a sensible boy; he had not shown impatience with his virgin bride who understandably knew little or nothing about sex. He would teach her in good time. Parvati joined her small family for breakfast satisfied with what she had seen.

At the breakfast table, things hadn't really changed over the years. Hari Mohan Pandey still preferred a heavy English breakfast: glass of orange juice, cornflakes with milk, bacon and eggs, toast with butter and marmalade, and coffee. All this was accompanied by a flash and tinkle of forks and knives, spoons and china. He ended his morning meals by lighting his briar pipe. Madan Mohan, on the other hand, still insisted on North Indian vegetarian food: pooris and *aalo-sabzi* made in ghee, or paranthas with pickle and *dahi*; and always milk instead of tea or coffee. At the end of his meals one of the servants brought him a finger bowl, since he ate with his fingers. Only Parvati Pandey's eating habits had changed, and reflected her slightly confused state, caught as she was between husband and son. Since Madan Mohan's early teens, she too had begun to share his Indian breakfast, best eaten

life's horoscope

with the fingers. Hari Mohan had shouted at her the first few times, but gradually reconciled himself to having lost his authority to the younger male. Now Parvati went back to Western food and cutlery only occasionally, when she felt sorry for her husband or wanted him to know that she still loved him, or when she wanted something from him.

Mohini was faced with a tricky situation at the breakfast table. Should she defer to her father-in-law or her husband? Should she first try and prove that she could handle forks and knives (which she could not with ease, but had got her friend Alice Carvalho from college to teach her) and then switch permanently to Indian food and use her fingers? The issue was decided for her when her mother-in-law instructed the servants to serve *Bade Sahib* the usual and everyone else poori-aaloo. They all ate in silence.

The day went by receiving another stream of visitors who came to congratulate the Pandeys bearing wedding gifts. So it went on till late in the evening. Mohini avoided eye contact with her husband and clung to her mother-in-law like a dutiful bahu. It was only after dinner that the couple were left alone for the night in their bedroom.

Mohini was still sulking. She took a bath,

changed into a fresh cotton sari and lay down on the bed, facing the wall. Madan also took a bath, changed into kurta-pyjamas and lay down on his side of the bed. After a while he stretched out his hand and put it on Mohini's shoulder. 'This is no way to behave towards your husband,' he said gently. She shrugged his hand off and replied, 'You don't want to have anything to do with me for three days. So I will talk to you when your silly period of abstinence is over.'

'But we *must* talk. You must tell me about yourself; you can ask me whatever you want to know about me. We are strangers to each other. We can become better acquainted, become friends, then lovers. This is laid down in the shastras; we must obey them.'

Mohini turned around to face him. There were tears in her eyes. 'What do you want to hear about me? I am a poor teacher's daughter. I've been to school and college. You did not like my winning a beauty contest. You don't want to see what I look like till three days are over. I don't understand you.' She covered her face with her hands and started sobbing.

Madan Mohan slid over to her side of the bed,

life's horoscope

gently took her hands off her face and wiped her tears. He kissed her on the forehead. 'You are a very pretty girl,' he said in a soothing voice. 'I don't have to see you naked to see how beautiful you are. The gods have made you what you are. I am lucky to have you as my wife.' Mohini clung to him. Gradually her sobs came to an end. She fell asleep in her husband's arms. Her body touched his many times during the night but made no demands on him.

Mohini regained her cheerfulness. She helped her mother-in-law and the servants in the kitchen, laying the table, receiving visitors, getting flowers from the garden and putting them in vases. The short crisis in her relationship with her husband was over. One more night and the period of sex taboo would also end. At long last she would get what she had been looking forward to since her engagement.

*

Came the night of all nights. After her mother-in-law left the couple in their bedroom, Mohini had a bath, liberally sprinkled her body with fragrant talcum powder, rubbed her gums with toothpaste vigorously, and came out looking as radiant as a bride should look for the event. Madan Mohan was pleased with what he saw and asked her to wait a few minutes till he too had had a bath. He scrubbed himself, brushed his teeth, and as a final touch, dabbed some French perfume on his neck and in his armpits—this last was a compromise he was constrained to make since *ittar*, the local perfume, was an invention of the Mughals, who were more abhorrent to him than the Whites. He joined Mohini on the sofa. He took two betel leaves wrapped in silver paper, put one in his mouth and the other in hers.

'So,' he said, and fell silent.

'So,' she replied, smiling through her betel-stained teeth. They held hands. 'So, Professor sahib, Panditji, my *Pati Parmeshwar*, I am happy to be your wife. You command, I obey.'

'I will begin with a kiss.' He meant to startle her with his repertoire of the many varieties of kisses described in the *Kamasutra*. But Mohini overpowered him.

'You can have as many as you want,' she replied and glued her lips to his.

They stayed in a tight embrace for a long time. Then Madan Mohan tried to regain control. He

life's horoscope

kissed her all over her face. His hands strayed to her bosom. He was not sure if she would like him taking that liberty with her. She undid the buttons of her blouse and the clasp of her bra. 'Kiss me here,' she whispered in his ear. Madan Mohan felt his control over the proceedings slipping; he had to assert himself, but the sight of her breasts made him go weak in the knees. He had only seen women's breasts in pictures and on marble statues, never in the flesh. He slobbered over them, not knowing which one of the two demanded more attention. 'They are beautiful,' he said hoarsely. 'I am not surprised you were chosen the beauty queen.'

'So you approve of the Western practice after all,' she laughed. 'Let me tell you, it is not only the bosom that matters in beauty contests. They measure the waist, buttocks, legs, everything. I came tops in every department.'

'Show me,' Madan Mohan said and then wondered who had spoken those words.

Mohini stood up, unwrapped her sari, freed herself of her blouse and bra and after a coy pause, undid the cord of her petticoat and let it slip down to the floor. She covered her sex with both her hands and turned around to let him see her smooth, well-rounded buttocks. Then she faced him and spread out her arms. 'Let's lie down.'

Madan Mohan recoiled in horror. What was that tuft of ugly black hair doing between her legs! He had not seen any such growth in the illustrated copies of the *Kamasutra* nor on any marble statues. He had hair above his genitals, yes, but wasn't that a masculine phenomenon? Why should a comely woman, a mrigini, have pubic hair? He was confused; also worked up. This was not going as he had planned. Mohini took his hand and led him to the nuptial bed. 'Take your clothes off. I want to see as much of you as you see of me,' she ordered. Meekly he obeyed her command. And revealed that he too had ugly black hair in his middle. For some reason nature had put it there. He was too worked up to ponder over the inscrutable phenomenon. They clasped each other in a tight embrace, and tumbled onto the bed. There followed a storm of kisses. It was time for the real act to begin. Madan Mohan explored his young bride's thighs with his hands and whispered in her ear: 'My little doe, this will hurt you, but only the first time. Then you will get used to it and enjoy it. Trust me.' While he was still fumbling, not knowing where to enter her,

life's horoscope

Mohini grasped his member and directed it to the right course. Madan Mohan recalled Vatsyayana's warning to be very gentle with a virgin. 'Go on, push it in,' Mohini said impatiently. Madan Mohan's head was now on fire; he had barely touched the opening of her vagina when he came in violent spurts all over her thighs.

For him it was a beautiful experience. Not for her. She could not hold back her frustration. She grabbed him by his hair and swore, '*Gadha*! Donkey! I haven't even begun and you've finished!' She extricated herself from under him and ran into the bathroom to clean herself and cool off. When she came out, she was confronted by an astonishing sight. Madan Mohan was standing on his head, with his limp penis hanging down like a stubby arrow pointing to his face.

'What are you doing?' she screamed.

'*Bindu* is the life force of a man. It's made of ingredients taken from all parts of his body, from his skull to his toes. To replenish it a man should do a *sirsh-asana* after he has had sex,' he explained from the position he was in.

'You call that having sex? You should have done it with your head, that might have been more satisfying,' she said in a huff. She lay down on her end of the double bed and switched off the lights.

Madan Mohan lowered his legs and sat up. He groped in the dark to get to the bathroom, washed himself and groped his way back to the bed. Sleep did not come to him for a long time. He pondered over where he had gone wrong. The *Kamasutra* had not prepared him for such crass behaviour on the part of a wife. Could she belong to a different category of women than he had presumed from her small size? He looked around the darkened room. Perhaps there was something wrong with their bedroom. He should consult Vaastu, which explained how houses should be built, rooms arranged, furniture placed. He had also not paid attention to the ancient science of gemology: gem stones were said to affect functions of the body. Some could rouse passions, others cool them down. His mind went forward and backward on the wisdom of the ancient texts and on his own failure to meet his newly married wife's expectations. Gradually sleep overtook him.

He did not see Mohini get up. He heard her splashing water in the bathroom and realized she had been up for some time. The bathroom door

life's horoscope

opened and she stepped out stark naked, rubbing her body with a towel. She was indeed a beautiful girl with hair hanging down to her waist and a perfect body, except for the indecent tuft of hair around her vagina. Couldn't she do something about that, and about her crassness? She had laid out her sari, petticoat and blouse on the bed. By way of greeting she said, '*Saara chippak-chippak*—sticky all over—belly, thighs, all chippak-chippak. I had to soap myself three times to get it off.' She changed into her clothes, touched his feet perfunctorily as he lay and went down to greet his parents.

Madan Mohan got up and went into the bathroom. While bathing he noticed some chippak-chippak on his groin and thighs as well. What a waste of precious bindu, he thought. It should have gone inside Mohini to give birth to a new life. His ears burned with the memory of the night's encounter. He changed into a fresh dhoti-kurta and joined the family waiting for him to have breakfast.

While the servant was laying the breakfast table, Madan Mohan's mother slipped upstairs to inspect her son's bed. She noticed a few drops of dried semen but no blood. She was mystified. She came back looking thoughtful.

The family was seated at the breakfast table. Madan Mohan and his father were having an animated dialogue. It started by Madan Mohan asking his father, 'Pitaji, did you consult a Vaastu expert when you had this bungalow designed?'

'An expert in what?' asked the father.

'Vaastu Shastra. You know, the ancient Hindu text on architecture and interior designing.'

'Never heard of it. I got a good architect to design this house. Of course he consulted me on my requirements. I think he did a good job. What's wrong with it?'

'No, no, I didn't say anything is wrong with our house. Only, Vaastu takes into account sun and wind movements. It is very particular about the direction in which a house faces, where the kitchen and lavatories should be located—that sort of thing.'

'He designed it in a way we could get the most of the sun in winter and the least in summer. Which way a house faces makes not the slightest difference.'

'It does. Vaastu says so. Our Sangathan office opened to the south. Our membership dropped. A Vaastu expert told us to change our entrance to the east and our membership picked up.'

'Rubbish! What kind of nonsense is this? What

life's horoscope

happens to hundred-storeyed skyscrapers going up in big cities abroad—not all of them face east.'

Madan Mohan had not worked that out but he was not the one to give up an argument easily. 'We don't know what happens to people living in houses facing south. But we can't discount ancient learning in so off-hand a manner. Vaastu goes into great detail not only about kitchens and toilets but also bedrooms, reception rooms, puja rooms, verandahs. It also specifies which direction the entrance and exit should face. Our ancestors followed all those rules.'

'Of course they had to,' snapped his father. 'They had *chulhas* which sent up smoke, so a kitchen had to be at the back. They shat in smelly pans which had to be cleaned by outcaste sweepers, so they had to be at some distance from their dwellings. We use electricity or gas for cooking, we have flush toilets which do not smell. We have air-conditioners to keep the house cool in summer and heaters to warm it in winter. Did your aastu-vaastu or whatever you call it know about these modern amenities?'

The argument was getting hot. It was bad to argue when eating. Parvati cut it short. 'Beta, will you be home for lunch?'

'I don't think so, Ma. I may be late at the Sangathan office. I have not been there for three days and there may be lots of work pending. Don't wait for me.'

'You've only been married three days. You should have taken some leave. Married couples take ten to fifteen days off for their honeymoon.'

'Honeymoon! A Western notion,' scoffed Madan Mohan. 'Did our forefathers go on honeymoons with their brides? To them dharma came first. The Sangathan is my dharma.'

The staff at the Sangathan office were surprised to see him. They too believed that he would be away for a week or ten days, in Kashmir or Shimla or some other hill resort, to get to know his bride better. They had not fixed any speaking schedule for him. Madan Mohan Pandey was as unpredictable as ever. He acknowledged his colleagues' felicitations and then added, 'Don't fix any speaking engagements for me till I ask for them. I have some ancient books to consult, so don't let anyone disturb me.'

He gave his assistant a list of books on Vaastu and Feng shui and asked him to get them from the office library. He spent the day going over them, making sketches of his bedroom, putting crosses

life's horoscope

indicating directions as on a mariner's map, and marking the way beds, sofas and chairs should be placed according to Vaastu shastra. Feng shui did not add much to his information. He was happy to be following instructions of a manual entirely conceived by India's great forefathers.

He got back home earlier than usual. The servants told him that his parents had taken their daughter-in-law to show her the sights of Delhi and would be back before sunset. Just as well, he thought, he wouldn't be disturbing anyone. He took the chart he had made up to his bedroom and ordered the servants to change the furniture around according to his instructions. The double bed had its head towards the north: exactly the opposite of what was prescribed in Vaastu. He had it turned around. The sofa was put alongside the bay window, the armchairs placed facing it across the round glass table with the flower vase. The servants did not question their young master; they had implicit faith in his mother's judgement that he was a *mahavidwan*, a man of great wisdom.

It was dark by the time the rest of the family returned from their sightseeing tour. Madan Mohan's father had planned the itinerary: to start with, the

Qutab Minar, followed by Humayun's tomb, ending at Nizamuddin's *dargah*. Mohini was very excited with what she had seen. 'They didn't allow us to go up the Minar,' she informed her husband. 'A young couple had jumped off it and killed themselves only two days ago. But I'm sure one would get a great view of the city from so high up in the sky.' Madan responded sourly, 'Yes, ruins all around. The walls of Prithviraj Chauhan's fort. And did you see the Quwwat-ul-Islam Mosque? Twenty-seven Hindu and Jain temples were destroyed to make one mosque. Not one, not two, but twenty-seven temples,' he repeated slowly. 'It is enough to make the blood of any Hindu boil with rage.'

His father bit his lip, took time to refill his pipe with tobacco, lit it and took a couple of puffs before he said in a tone of suppressed rage, 'We went sightseeing, not to raise our blood pressures.'

Mohini sensed a storm brewing between father and son and quickly changed the subject. 'Surely you can't say anything against Nizamuddin Auliya; he loved both Hindus and Muslims. We saw a lot of Hindu families at the dargah. They were asking for favours and tying *mannat* strings around the marble trellis of the tomb.'

life's horoscope

'*Bewakoofs*. They were a bunch of fools,' said Madan Mohan.

'I also tied a mannat string,' confessed Mohini.

'You are a bewakoof too!'

'It's no use arguing with him,' the father intervened. 'By his reckoning everyone except he is a bewakoof.'

'You should read our true history and not the Muslim and Christian versions, Pitaji. You will continue to believe in the lies of the barbarians otherwise.'

'Bas, bas, enough of this,' said Parvati firmly, waving her hands to drive away clouds of ill will. 'You make a mountain out of a mole hill. Mohini enjoyed her outing—didn't you, beta? Next time we will take her to the Birla Mandir, the Hanuman Mandir and Bangla Sahib Gurdwara.'

Madan Mohan's exchange of words with his father cast a gloom over the rest of the evening. No one was in the mood to talk at dinner; they gobbled up the food laid on the table. Hari Mohan Pandey left for his study without bidding anyone goodnight. He was followed by his wife and then Mohini. Madan Mohan felt guilty for having spoilt the atmosphere. But how could he help it if just about anything he said or did irritated his father? And his new wife—she did not seem interested in anything he stood for. It would take him a long while to bring her around to his ideal of a good Hindu wife. With a heavy heart he went up to his bedroom. Worse awaited him.

Mohini was reprimanding the servants for turning around the bed and furniture without consulting her. 'Bahuji, Chhotey Sahib ordered us to do so.' Just then the Chhotey Sahib entered the room. Mohini turned on him. 'What is all this *ootpataang*? Without asking me, without telling me.' The servants waited nervously for further orders. 'What do you mean?' responded Madan Mohan sharply. 'There is nothing nonsensical about it. This is how the interior of a bedroom should be according to Vaastu Shastra. Nothing goes right in a house or a room that is wrongly designed or laid out.' Before the servants could leave, Mohini spat out the venom that had built up in her: 'When you don't know how to dance, you blame the dance floor,' she shouted the Hindi proverb. Madan Mohan was crushed; his manhood had been questioned in front of his own servants. Mohini realized what she had blurted out and covered her face and broke into

life's horoscope

sobs. She rushed to the bathroom and slammed the door behind her. The servants slipped out of the room.

Madan Mohan lay down on his bed, utterly defeated and deflated. He did not change into his night clothes. He just kept staring at the ceiling. He heard Mohini come out of the bathroom and lie down on the bed. They did not speak to each other. Neither had any desire to get closer to the other. They slept fitfully. At some point shortly after midnight, Madan Mohan awoke in a panic; it was a dream he had had, but he could remember nothing of it. He lay awake for a while, looking at Mohini, asleep, facing the wall. If he could rouse his lust, he thought, he might break through the wall that separated them. He fixed his gaze on her buttocks, dimly visible in the moonlight streaming in through the open window. Nothing happened. He put a hand inside his pyjamas and fondled his penis, but it remained limp as a snail. His panic rose. This was a calamity he had not foreseen; the *Kamasutra* had said nothing about penises that failed to respond. What if Mohini found out? Uncouth woman that she was, she might shout this out to the whole world! He stiffened, afraid of making any movement that might wake her up, and prayed for sleep. An hour, the longest of his life, passed before his prayer was answered.

Madan Mohan did not know when Mohini got up in the morning. He did not hear her bathing. By the time he opened his eyes, she was quietly shutting the door behind her to join his parents. He went to the bathroom to take a shower. He noticed what looked like a blob of cotton wool soaked in blood floating in the toilet. Did Mohini suffer from piles at this young age? He was puzzled. He went downstairs. His mother was in the puja room, saying her morning prayers. His father was in his study, reading the morning papers. Mohini was sitting alone. Madan asked her, 'Aren't you doing puja this morning?' She shook her head and replied, 'I can't go to the puja room for a few days.' He could not see why, but did not ask her. When his mother came out and went to the kitchen to organize breakfast, Mohini did not join her as she did every morning. 'Aren't you going to help Ma with the breakfast?' he asked. Mohini again shook her head and replied, 'Not for four or five days.'

'Why?'

'Because I'm not clean,' she replied with exasperation.

'Not clean? But you've just had a bath.'

Mohini snarled, '*Buddhoo!*'

Madan Mohan was taken aback. Yet another snub, and first thing in the morning. It was after breakfast during which his mother did most of the talking that Madan Mohan had a few moments alone with her. 'Ma, what is wrong with Mohini? I only asked her why she did not do her puja or help in the kitchen and she abused me. She called me a fool. Is this the sort of language a Hindu wife should use for her husband?'

His mother was overcome with emotion. She put her arm round her son's shoulders. 'How innocent you are, beta.' Then she proceeded to quickly explain the workings of a woman's body. How was it, wondered Madan Mohan, that the Hindu classics he had read had not informed him of these things?

Instead of being cheered by the contribution his mother had made to his knowledge of the world, Madan Mohan went into deep depression. Despite the academic distinctions he had amassed, his father did not have much of an opinion of him. He had failed as a teacher in college, and he knew what he said at the shakha meetings was beyond the comprehension of bania shopkeepers. And there was Mohini, from a lower middle-class family, half-baked product of a convent and a Christian college, who had the audacity to call him a donkey and a fool. She had no refinement; she would never make the ideal wife. He was fairly sure her unscrupulous parents had given him a false horoscope for her. He did not want to have anything more to do with her. If she wanted to live with him, he would let her do so but he would never again let her touch him.

Mohini's thoughts were equally dark. She had looked forward to being married to the only son of a well-to-do family who was reputed to be a scholar. She also expected him to be an ardent lover. She had eagerly awaited the night when she would surprise him with her perfect body and rouse him to great passion. But this fellow had turned out to be a crackpot who did not know the first thing about making love. He assessed her as some zoologist did an animal—a deer, an elephant. Her beauty was wasted on the fool. A sixty-year old would be more youthful than him. She did not want to have anything more to do with him. Her only fear was her parents' reaction. They believed that once a daughter was given away in marriage she only left her

life's horoscope

husband's home on a bier, wrapped in a red shroud signifying death in matrimonial bliss. She resolved to confront them. And if she failed, she would look for a job as a teacher in some school or college. She had the requisite qualifications.

The atmosphere in the Pandey household was tense. The one voice heard when the family was together for meals was that of the mother. Others rarely answered her questions. Mohini was anyhow due to return to her parents' for a few days, as was customary, and await her husband's first visit to his in-laws' home to fetch her.

A week later, Mohini's brother came to Delhi to escort his sister to Mathura. Weeks passed, then months. Madan Mohan did not go to Mathura to bring her back. Gradually both the Pandeys and the Joshis resigned themselves to the fact that the marriage had ended without being consummated.

'What wrong did we do to deserve this blot on our family's reputation?' Parvati asked her husband after he had lit his briar pipe one morning. He did not answer her question and continued to draw on his pipe and fill the air with fragrant smoke. She waved away the smoke with one hand and repeated her question. 'Where did we go wrong, I ask you.

We had their horoscopes matched, they assured us of a happy marriage with lots of grandchildren. Madan himself examined them and approved of the girl. Tell me, what do you think went wrong?' she said demanding an answer.

Pandey Senior put down his pipe on the table and snapped, 'That boy is a gadha. He is an impotent fool!'

Parvati Pandey sank back in her chair, covered her face with her hands and sobbed, 'How can you be so coarse about your only child? Shame on you!' Then she regained her composure, sat up and said defiantly, 'You wait and watch. My son is a mahavidwan. With his wisdom and learning he will become a great leader of our country!'

'God save our country,' said Hari Mohan Pandey and returned to his pipe.

zora singh

They knew him by different names. To his Sikh admirers he was *Panth Rattan*, Jewel of the Community; his Urdu-speaking friends named him *Fakhr-e-millat*, Pride of the Nation. He was also *Nar Aadmee*, He Man, and *Doston ka Dost*, The Greatest of Friends. Those who did not like him called him *Khushaamdee Tattoo*: Flattering Jackass. They often described him as a *chamcha*, a sycophantic hanger-on, and said he was *chaalaak* (cunning), a *chaalbaaz* (an intriguer) and a *chaar sau bees* (a cheat). Since he made no secret of enjoying his sundowner and the company of fair women, other titles were also bestowed on him. He was a *sharaabee* (drunkard), *kabaabee* (great eater) and *randeebaaz* (whoremonger).

There was some truth in everything that was

said about Zora Singh to his face and behind his back. He was all things to all men. The Sikhs praised him because he was a devout Sikh who said his daily prayers. He was seen at the gurdwara very early each morning when he went to drop his wife there, and could deliver sermons better than any preacher. Once he was persuaded to read the marriage vows at a Sikh wedding. He was lucid and convincing. He told the bridegroom, 'Hereafter you will look upon every other woman as a mother, sister or daughter.' And to the bride he said, 'And you, my daughter, will look upon all men besides your husband as your brothers.' In conclusion he said, 'The Great Guru will bless your union as long as you remain faithful to each other.' The congregation was impressed by his oration and many came forward to congratulate him. However, two nasty men with nasty minds took him aside. One said, 'All that you said was beautifully said, Zora, but it did not behove you to say it.' The other, who was nastier, asked him, 'Yaar Zora, how many mothers and sisters have you fucked since you got married?'

Though Zora Singh was known to be religious, he also had the reputation of being a womanizer.

zora singh

Some people found this hard to believe. Whenever Zora and his wife Eeshran went to parties, he had his arm around her shoulder. He always introduced her as 'my better half' or 'my Home Minister' in a tone as though he had invented these terms. He paid her all the attention a loving husband would to his wife. Eeshran never had any complaints, nor indeed did she believe that he could ever be unfaithful to her. He was an ideal husband, and a good father to their two sons. She did not resent his going to all-male *mujra* parties where the only women present were professional dancing and singing girls. At the end of the evening the host offered the pick of the girls to Zora, as he was usually the most important guest. Zora was too much of a gentleman to refuse the honour; he spent an hour with the girl in the room assigned to them. Eeshran never complained. After all, mujras were a hallowed Indian tradition and never regarded by Indian women as a violation of their matrimonial rights.

Deepo, however, was a different matter.

Deepo was the wife of Zora's office peon, Tota Singh, who had been run over and killed by a speeding truck while on his way home one evening. Zora had heard of his having left behind a young widow and two children. Apart from the compensation given to her by the court, Zora had her employed as a cleaning woman-cum-chaprasi in his office and allowed her to carry on living in the staff quarters allotted to her late husband. Deepo had passed her tenth standard exam and could sign her name on mail that required acknowledgement of receipt. She was twenty-five, and dark and strongly built, like any Punjabi peasant girl. She had taken her husband's death very badly and was often seen wiping her tears with her dupatta while sitting on the stool outside the Sahib's office. Zora felt very sorry for her and was very concerned. Two months after the tragedy he called on her in the staff quarters with toys for her sons. He meant to offer Deepo some paternal advice on what to do with her life. 'Deepo, you are still very young. Why don't you get married again?' he asked tenderly.

'Sahibji, who will marry a widow with two children? I can't even bear children any more—both Tota and I had our *nasbandi* after our second child. Who will want to marry a barren woman?'

Deepo sat down on her haunches, put her head on Zora's feet and sobbed, 'Sahibji, I have no one left in the world besides you. And I have nothing to

zora singh

give in return for your kindness. I feel ashamed. You are my God and provider, I am your servant. I can only render *seva* to you.'

Deepo's boys were out playing with their new toys. Zora was overcome with emotion. He bolted the door from the inside and took a very willing Deepo on her creaking charpai.

This became a weekly routine. Deepo awaited the Sahib's two words: '*Aj shaam*, this evening.' She would go home early, take a bath, send the boys out to play and await her lord and master. On Zora's part it was kindness towards a helpless widow, who might otherwise have become easy prey to other men's lust or turned into a harlot. For Deepo, it was giving thanks to a man who provided for her and her family.

It would have been unfair to malign Zora as a womanizer on this count.

There was also much gossip about Zora having promoted men in his department after they had made their wives accessible to him. But he never put any pressure on his subordinates to bring their wives to him. They came of their own accord—often to pay their respects to his wife Eeshran, as was customary—and if he happened to be at home at the time, plead with him to keep a kindly eye on their husbands' future. From the coquettish way some of these women behaved it was clear to Zora that neither they nor their husbands would be averse to his obliging them. So he would call on the women in the afternoons when their husbands were in the office and their children at school. One visit or two was all he paid them, then promoted their husbands or transferred them to posts they desired. It caused no heartache or ill will except to those who were superseded, and it was they who went around spreading the ugly rumour that Zora helped only those whose wives he had slept with. This was only partially true, and did not justify his being labelled a womanizer—certainly not in his own eyes, nor in the eyes of his wife Eeshran, who looked upon her husband as a godsend: manly, handsome, capable, kind, god-loving, noble, and one who did his 'homework', as he called it, whenever she wanted it done.

Zora had done no harm to anyone and was often puzzled when he heard that people spread nasty stories about him. One evening at the Golf Club, one of the four he played with remarked in a jocular manner, 'Zora, you are the biggest chaar sau

zora singh

bees I've ever met in my life.' The fellow had just lost a lot of money to Zora and his partner (Zora almost always won because he was a good golfer with a low handicap and had a ball-spotter—*aageyvaala*—who discreetly moved the ball with his foot from an awkward lie to the top of a tuft of grass). The remark stung him. He pondered on it on his way home and was somewhat depressed. He told Eeshran about it. She tried to cheer him up. 'Take no notice of what that foul-mouthed fellow says; it's just envy. See where he is today, close to retirement and only an executive engineer. And you still have six or seven years left in service and are chief engineer—the first Indian to become one! He burns with jealousy. I spit on his face—*thhoo*!'

There was much to envy about Zora Singh. His father had raised money to send him to the Imperial Engineering College in London to get a degree where he had been an instant hit with his fellow students and professors. He'd played field hockey, cricket and tennis for his college, and had been good at his studies. He was elected president of his college union. To his Indian friends he gave good advice: 'If you want to get on with the English, follow the rule of three Fs: fuck, feed and flatter.'

He did his share of the first; he was generous when it came to buying beer for his friends; and he had a honeyed tongue and was subtle in his compliments— he sensed that the English were put off by blatant flattery. He got his engineering degree and sat for the competitive exam for the Imperial Engineering Service the first year it was thrown open to Indians. Some examiners were from his college, two of them on the panel of interviewers. He was the only candidate, English or Indian, to be awarded full marks in the viva voce. He sailed into the Imperial Service; the two other Indians who made the grade were way behind him.

So Zora began his career as an engineer in India receiving the same salary and fringe benefits as his English colleagues. Like all bachelors in the ICS he was greatly sought after by those who had marriageable daughters. His parents arranged his marriage with the only daughter of the leading Sikh lawyer of Lahore. The one condition they put to the girl's parents, very subtly, was that they expected to be compensated for the money they had spent on their son's education in England. This was readily agreed to. After a lavish wedding, Eeshran moved into a small government bungalow allotted to her husband and furnished by her parents, in a sparsely inhabited upcoming town which was to become the capital of India, New Delhi.

Zora and Eeshran were well-matched and shared much in common. Most important was attachment to their faith, Sikhism. Eeshran brought a copy of the holy scripture, the Granth Sahib, as part of her dowry. Zora set up a prayer room in which it was installed on a lectern-shaped desk and draped with expensive silk. They called it *Babaji da Kamra*, the room of the Holy Father. Though Zora proclaimed loudly that Sikhism disapproved of idol worship, he and his wife revered their holy book much the same way as Hindus did their idols. During the summer they had the ceiling fan whirring round the clock; during winter they wrapped the Granth in cashmere shawls. They did not regard it as idol worship but as respect due to a book of profound spiritual wisdom. They took turns opening the book in the early hours of the morning and reading a few pages from it. They put it to rest before they had their evening meal. On his way to the office, Zora dropped Eeshran off at Gurdwara Bangla Sahib. An hour later his car came to take her home. In the evenings they went to Lodhi Gardens for a brisk walk. Wherever they were invited they went together, and to all the world they seemed to be living examples of the perfect married couple—*ek jyot duey moortee*, one light in two bodies.

Zora got on very well with his English colleagues and bosses. He was good at his work and a hard taskmaster when it came to dealing with building contractors. There were hundreds of things to be built before New Delhi was fit to be the capital of India—new roads, clerks' and officers' flats, bridges across the river Yamuna, an airport, railway stations, secretariats, a Parliament House and Viceregal lodge, among other things. Building contracts were up for grabs. Zora scrutinized all the tenders made by contractors, lowered the figures and paid regular visits to the construction sites. Contractors were eager to be on his right side. Gora Sahibs did not accept bribes—and what Zora took were not bribes but his commission, as did all his Indian subordinates, without compromising on the quality of the work. This was not regarded as corruption; it was, as Zora put it, *Ooperwaley di deyn*, a gift from above. It added up to more than ten times his salary every month. And it was tax free.

The sahibs knew that Indians took commissions

zora singh

and that Zora was no exception. But while they looked down on the others with contempt they treated Zora with respect. He was a go-getter and got things done on time. He did not grovel before them as other Indians did but behaved with dignity and kept a respectable distance from them. On Christmas Day, when others came loaded with baskets of goodies and crates of Scotch, their gifts were grudgingly accepted but the chaprasis were ordered to send them away. Zora, on the other hand, who only brought one bottle, was invited to share a drink.

Zora got promotions out of turn. Before he was thirty he was made superintending engineer and conferred the title of Sardar Sahib. Five years later he was made executive engineer and conferred the title of Sardar Bahadur. By then he had bought three plots of land which were available at very low prices. On one he built a large house for his years after retirement, then two others to earn rental income to supplement his pension. The houses cost him almost nothing. Building contractors who were obliged to him provided labour and material free of cost. He designed the houses and supervised their building in his spare time. He did not rob anyone of their honestly earned money, only allowed people who owed their prosperity to him to pay their debts of gratitude.

As time drew near for the British to leave India, people began to say that the days of Zora's prosperity were numbered. They were mistaken. Zora was elected president of the Imperial Golf Club and the Gymkhana Club—not by the English but by a majority of Indian members. He had hoped that before they departed the British would confer a knighthood on him as they had on a succession of Englishmen who had become Chief Engineers. He was disappointed when, in the final honours list issued by them, he found he had been fobbed off with a mere OBE. Indians no longer cared for Sardar Sahibs and Sardar Bahadurs, and most didn't even know what OBE or CIE stood for, but a Sir was a Sir and they all respected that—whether they were lackeys of the British or followers of Gandhi.

Those who were certain that a man like Zora would be cut to size as soon as India had its own government, were in for a surprise. Zora knew his countrymen better than they. The day the name of the Minister of Works was announced, Zora was amongst the dozens who called on him to pay his

zora singh

respects. When he was shown in he touched the Minister's feet and said, 'Your humble servant's name is Zora Singh. I am your Chief Engineer of public works. Sir, it will be my privilege to work under your guidance. Your wish will be my command.'

The Minister sized him up, looking from turban to toe, before he responded. 'Zora Singhji, I have gone through your personal file. It is very favourable. You are said to be a good worker who does the task assigned to him before schedule. We have a lot of new buildings to make. Colonies for millions of refugees who have been driven out of Pakistan, new commercial centres and what not. You must see me every day to report on the progress you are making. I don't want the Prime Minister to have any complaints against any department in my Ministry.'

Zora also sized up his Minister. He was an ugly, dark man with thick lips and podgy fingers, on four of which he wore gold rings studded with precious stones prescribed by his astrologer. He was from Orissa, and the only one of his tribe to have gone to college. Being from an underprivileged community he freely enjoyed the special privileges generously bestowed on him by the Gandhi-inspired government.

The Minister was known to have quite an appetite for women. It was said that when he had been Health Minister in Orissa, he wanted a nurse or a lady doctor every evening while he toured the districts. And when he became Education Minister it was a lady teacher. Now he was in the Centre heading a ministry that had no women officers. Perhaps, Zora thought, he could arrange for one of the girls from the typing pool to go to the Minister's house for dictation whenever he so desired. After all, what the Minister wanted every woman had—whether she was a gazetted officer, a typist or a sweeperess. Zora had this at the back of his mind when he replied, 'Sir, I give you my word there will be no complaints against my department.'

Zora went about his work with greater zeal than ever before. Hundreds of contractors had to be engaged. They knew the rules of the game. For every building they paid a commission to Zora and his subordinates. Once a week Zora carried an envelope containing currency notes of a lakh or more and quietly put it on the Minister's table. Nothing was said about the contents of the envelope. Zora knew that the Minister wanted cash to fight his elections and keep his family in comfort. Since the

Minister could not clear his desk of files before he left for home in the evening, Zora ordered the head of the typing pool to send one of the girls to the Minister's house after dinner, to take dictation. He did not let his Minister down. The Minister also stood by him. When the government of independent India introduced honours, Zora was among the first to be awarded a Padma Vibhushan.

More honours followed. Zora was unanimously elected president of the Delhi Gurdwara Committee and headed the many schools, colleges and hospitals run by it. He organized an international Sikh conference to which he invited Sikhs who had been highly successful in various fields: one owned a whiskey distillery in the Highlands, another a historic castle in Ireland which came with a peerage, a few had become Members of the British and the Canadian Parliaments, one had made it to the American Congress, a few were judges of high courts of different countries and there were a dozen or more who had risen from nothing to become millionaires. Zora got his Minister to persuade the Prime Minister to inaugurate the three-day conference. Foreign participants were honoured with shawls, yellow turbans and *kirpans*. For three days the World Sikh

Conference made the front pages of Indian newspapers.

Zora had not done all this for nothing. He discreetly managed to get the richest and most famous American Sikh to say something about his service to the community at the concluding session. After Zora had made his final oration lauding the great contribution of the Sikhs to the prosperity and defence of India, the American NRI spoke on behalf of the foreign delegates. He presented Zora a silver kirpan with a handle made of gold studded with precious stones. Zora drew it out of its sheath and shouted the Sikh war cry, '*Boley so Nihaal!*' The crowd responded, '*Sat Sri Akaal.*' The American NRI concluded his speech with words addressed to Zora Singh: 'I know I am expressing the sentiments of the entire Sikh community living in India and abroad when I say, Zora Singh, we honour you with the title of *Panth Rattan*—Jewel of the Khalsa nation.'

There was a thunderous applause with resounding cries of '*Boley so Nihal*; *Sat Sri Akaal!*' Zora Singh was overcome with emotion. He joined the palms of his hands and bowed deeply. There were tears streaming down his face.

zora singh

Zora had one year left for retirement. His sons were, as they say, gainfully employed, one as manager of a large tea estate in Assam with a huge bungalow and a big salary, the other as an executive with a British-Marwari firm producing and marketing paints. They had said they would choose their own wives. Though neither Zora nor his wife believed in the caste system, they hoped the girls they married would be from good Jat Sikh families like theirs. Eeshran also looked forward to moving into the home Zora had built and spending their remaining days in prayer, going on pilgrimages to historic Sikh shrines and listening to keertan.

Zora had other plans.

Next to the Prime Minister, his Minister was the most powerful man in the cabinet and informally acknowledged as the PM's deputy. He presided over cabinet meetings when the Prime Minister was visiting foreign countries, which was often. The Minister owed a lot to Zora for keeping him afloat in politics. In return he had done his best to promote Zora professionally. They were no longer Minister and civil servant but what people called *jigree dost*, the closest of friends.

Zora gave his Minister an expensive birthday

gift every year. This year he decided to outdo himself. He went to the leading jewellers in the city and asked them to make a special ring for him— platinum with a blue star-sapphire, the largest and best they had. It cost almost five lakhs. He paid for it in cash. Before he quit office, Zora had one last favour to ask of his friend.

There was always a large crowd to wish the Minister on his birthday. Zora told the secretary he would like to see the Minister alone. He was told to come at 6.30 p.m., when all the others would have left and it was time for the Minister to go home. Zora arrived a few minutes before the appointed time and was ushered into the Minister's retiring room. He heard the Minister thank his many well-wishers and bid them farewell. When he came into his private room to pick up some files Zora was there waiting for him. They embraced each other warmly. '*Mubarak*! *Mubarak*! May you live another hundred years,' thundered Zora with great feeling, 'the country needs a man like you at the helm to march towards prosperity.'

'*Bas, bas*, Zora. You don't have to flatter me. We are friends,' replied the Minister.

'Oh, but I'm not paying lip service; I mean

zora singh

every word of it. Ask any Indian in any walk of life and they'll say the same. You are the pride of India and its hope for the future.'

'Enough of this,' retorted the Minister. 'I must get home. My wife has arranged a birthday party for me.'

'Oh, I almost forgot my humble birthday gift,' said Zora feigning forgetfulness. He took the little red velvet box out of his pocket and gently pulled out the platinum and blue star-sapphire ring. 'Please let me have the honour of slipping it on your finger,' he said as he took one of the Minister's hands in his. Three fingers had rings on them. He slipped it on the fourth. It outshone all the other rings.

'Zora, this must have cost you a fortune,' said the Minister as he admired the new ring on his hand.

'Sir, nothing is good enough for you. It will remind you of your humble servant when he is no longer serving you. I know you will keep a benign eye on me after I retire in a few months' time.'

'Zora, the nation needs men like you. I will see to it that you continue to serve the country as long as you can.'

Three months later, Zora retired from service. A month after that, he was nominated member of the Rajya Sabha.

'What will this fellow do in Parliament?' scoffed his detractors.

They were in for a surprise.

Zora's maiden speech was a masterly performance, humility peppered with choice quotations from the scriptures—Hindu, Muslim, Christian and Sikh. He lauded the virtues of truth, honesty and righteous living. He paid fulsome compliments to his Minister and assured the members of the House that as long as there were men of his stature, ability and integrity, nothing would go wrong with India. He ended his stirring oration with a full-throated cry, '*Mera Bharat Mahaan*; Jai Hind!' The members rose together to applaud him. One after another they came to shake his hand.

While he was still being felicitated by fellow members, a Parliamentary orderly in a white, starched turban came and handed him a small note. The Minister wanted to see him in his chamber. Zora followed the orderly through the corridors of Parliament House and was ushered into the

zora singh

Minister's office. The Minister stood up and took both Zora's hands in his. '*Shaabaash*, well done! I heard everything you said. I am proud of you.'

'Sir, whatever I am, it is due to your kindness. Who else would have cared about an insignificant creature like me?'

The Minister ordered coffee. 'Zora, have you applied to the Parliament for a house? You are entitled to one, you know.'

'Sir, what will I do with another house? I have a few of my own.'

'All said and done, you are a simple-minded Sardar. *Kaam aayega*—it will come in handy. You don't have to live in it. Don't ask for one of those flats where the other MPs live. There are nice bungalows with large gardens away from the main road. The best are along two roads facing the India International Centre. The roads end with some school playgrounds. When the schools are closed there is no one around apart from the residents of those bungalows. Ask for one at the end of the road. I will make sure you get what you ask for. Zoraji, *Kaam aayega*,' he repeated.

It dawned on Zora what the Minister meant. 'Yes sir, I will go and apply for one right away.'

Zora's speech was covered on Doordarshan news. The next morning, his photographs were on the front page of every paper. One carried the caption 'Builder of buildings becomes builder of the nation'.

A new chapter began in Zora's life. With age his appetite for sex declined and his religious fervour increased. His weekly visits to Deepo became fortnightly, then monthly and then once every few months. Deepo never made any demands on him but complied with his wishes when he came to see her. There were times when he made no move to share her creaking charpai with her but just spent a few minutes talking to her. When Deepo was relieved from her job and told to vacate the government quarters, Zora gave her a room in his servants' quarters and the job of looking after his wife who had developed acute arthritis and had trouble walking. Deepo's sons had found jobs, one as an electrician, the other as a car mechanic, and shared a rented room in the suburbs.

Deepo fitted very well into Zora's household. She spent most of the day with Eeshran, helped her bathe and dress, combed her hair and pressed her legs when she was tired. She accompanied her master and mistress to the gurdwara every morning. While Zora went to play his round of golf, reduced now from eighteen holes to nine, the two women listened to keertan till he came to pick them up. When Parliament was in session Zora spent his mornings listening to questions and answers and often stayed on for coffee and snacks with MPs of both Houses in the Central Hall. He was nominated to several Parliamentary committees and made chairman of a couple of public corporations which carried the rank of Cabinet Minister, which in turn gave him the privilege of sporting a red light on the roof of his car. He celebrated his elevation to the House of Elders by buying a new car with a factory-fitted air-conditioner and sound system. At his request he was given the number plate he desired: DLH 1000. His friends gave him a new title, Zora Singh Hazaria, Commander of One Thousand.

Zora had no time for introspection. He knew full well that it would only make him unhappy without doing him any good. He had made money, lots of it on the side. So had all the other engineers. He had kept his Minister securely on his side by funding him and providing him with women. Their close association had earned handsome dividends for both. The Minister was ten years younger than him, and his lust for *naya maal*, fresh meat as he called it in English, had not abated. Zora provided him a safe place—his Parliamentary bungalow—to savour the joys of young female flesh for which Zora paid in cash. Zora, on his part, had frequently cheated on his wife, but had also taken good care of her and his family. There was little point in reflecting on his shortcomings and making himself miserable. This was the way of the world—Zora was a man of the world destined to fulfil his life's ambitions: wealth, respectability and honour. Whenever his conscience disturbed him he turned to prayer. The last thing he did before turning in for the night was to recite *ardaas*, naming the ten gurus, their 'living' emblem, the Granth Sahib, and asking them to forgive him for any sins he may have committed. He slept the sleep of the Just.

One afternoon, the Minister's private secretary rang Zora up to say that his boss wanted to speak to him, and put him on the line.

'Zora Singh at your service, sir. It must be Eid today—I will look out for the new moon!'

The Minister ignored the flattery and came to the point. 'Zoraji, will you be at home this evening?

zora singh

I have something important to discuss with you. Around 7 p.m.?'

'Sir, your wish is my command. It always has been, and will be to the end of my days. It will be an honour to have you step into my home. It has been a long time.'

Zora informed his wife and told her to have the sitting room carpets hoovered, put fresh flowers in the vases and have the air-conditioner switched on a couple of hours before the Minister was due to arrive. Eeshran was as excited as he. Both had an early evening bath and got into fresh clothes. A bottle of Blue Label Johnnie Walker, two cut glasses, two bottles of soda and a silver bucket of ice-cubes were laid out on the table.

The Minister's car pulled up at exactly 7 p.m. Zora and his wife went out to receive him. The Minister carried a large bouquet of yellow gladioli in his hand. His orderly had a basket of red roses. '*Behen* Eeshran, these are for you,' said the Minister handing her the bouquet. The orderly followed them indoors and placed the basket of roses on the table. Eeshran was overwhelmed by the gesture. '*Mantriji*, you should not have taken all this trouble. This is like your own home.'

'Eeshranji, nothing can be good enough for a noble lady like you. You must have performed some very good deed in your previous life to have found a husband like Zora. Let me tell you, he is one in a million. You are the luckiest woman on earth.'

Eeshran joined the palms of her hands and acknowledged, 'It is all the great Guru's kindness. Who are we but vermin crawling in the dirt.'

There was a moment of silence. Zora turned to the Minister. 'Sir, shall we do the *Bismillah*?' he asked picking up the bottle of Scotch.

'A very *chhota* one for me,' replied the Minister. 'I have many important files to go through tonight.' Eeshran sensed it was time to leave them alone. 'I will send some hot hot *pakoras* for you to enjoy with your drinks,' she said and left.

Zora handed the Minister his drink. They raised their glasses, clinked them: 'Jai Hind.'

The Minister did not waste any more time on preliminaries. 'Zoraji, tomorrow there will be a few questions in the Rajya Sabha concerning my ministry. One of them is about money that building contractors gave engineers when you were chief engineer. I will place my replies on the table of the

zora singh

House. I think it would be good if you made a statement after supplementaries have been answered.'

He handed Zora Singh a sheaf of pink papers with questions that would be raised in Parliament the next day. Zora glanced over them and was surprised to find one in particular. 'Sir, the fellow who has put forward this question is from your own party.'

The Minister gave him a broad smile. 'There is a conspiracy to malign me so that the new Prime Minister drops me from the Cabinet. You know he is still wet behind the ears and listens to all kinds of gossip. They are saying that I've been taking huge bribes, that I keep mistresses and drink heavily.'

'That is absolute *bakwaas*—rubbish!' responded Zora Singh. 'I'll make mincemeat of the bastard.'

The Minister smiled and patted Zora on the back. 'Not with anger but with cold facts and logic. Carry the House with you. And let that Prime Minister know whom he can trust and who are the rats that surround him.' Saying this, he got up. 'That's all I came to see you about.'

'Won't you have another one for the road? Eeshran, Mantriji is leaving. Come say Sat Sri Akaal to him.'

Eeshran hobbled in. 'Mantriji, when will you turn your blessed feet towards our humble abode again?'

'Behen Eeshran, whenever you order. I have only this one true friend in the world,' he replied as he stepped into his car.

*

Zora did not have his second drink nor eat much at dinner. 'What's the matter?' asked Eeshran. 'You seem to have lost your appetite; did Mantriji say something that upset you?'

'I have to speak in Parliament tomorrow. Some fellow has put forward questions insinuating that there was corruption in my department when I was chief engineer. I have to keep the facts ready. I'll have to look up old files and may be late. Before you go to bed ring up my steno and tell him to be here by 8 a.m. There may be a lot of typing to do.'

'May *Wahguru* place burning coals on the fellow's tongue!' said Eeshran. 'You have done nothing to be ashamed of. Let the world know what you have done for your country. Don't worry too much, Wahguru is with you.' She quoted a line from the scripture: 'When You are on my side, what fear need I have?'

zora singh

Zora went to his study and pulled out old files of newspaper clippings about building projects he had been involved in from the time of the British and since Independence. He flagged some and made notes he could use later. It was well after midnight when he joined Eeshran in the bedroom. She was still awake reading her prayer book. She shut it and said, 'You must sleep. One should be fresh and in good shape to take on one's enemies in battle.' Zora was too worked up to sleep soundly. In his mind he kept rehearsing the speech he had to deliver and hearing the applause that would follow.

Zora was up early next morning, had his bath, recited the morning prayer and read the day's message—*vaak*—from the Granth Sahib. It augured well: 'Whatever I ask of the Lord He gives the same in full measure.'

When the steno arrived, he asked him to take photocopies of the clippings he had selected. He rehearsed his speech again in subdued tones and was ready for the day. He arrived in Parliament House fifteen minutes before the question hour, signed his name in the attendance register, shook a few hands and took the seat allotted to him. He placed the files he had brought in front of him.

The hall began to fill up, the opposition benches faster than those of the ruling party. Zora looked up: the press and visitors' galleries were full. So was the officials' gallery where senior civil servants sat armed with files to brief ministers whenever required. Slowly the ministers began to arrive with their orderlies carrying their briefcases. And finally, the Prime Minister, who came to the Rajya Sabha only when questions concerning the departments under him had to be answered. He took his seat next to Zora's Minister.

As the clock struck eleven, the heralds announced the entry of the Vice President who was also Speaker of the House. The members rose and bowed before him. Without further ado he announced, 'Question number one.' The member who had put down the question stood up and repeated: 'Question number one'. The Minister concerned answered it as well as the supplementaries. The second question was dealt with in similar fashion. It was the third question that concerned Zora. The Minister stood up and replied, 'Papers have been laid on the table of the House.' A dozen hands from the opposition went up. Zora also put up his hand. The Speaker made a note of the names. The supplementaries were answered laconically by the Minister: 'Yes Sir, no Sir, does not arise.' The man who had raised the question was clearly very sheepish about having raised a hornet's nest and embarrassed the ruling party to which he belonged. The Speaker asked the leader of the opposition to ask his question. But instead of framing his question, the leader of the opposition launched into an angry rant about corruption in the Public Works Department and brandished copies of newspapers carrying stories of large sums being paid by building contractors to government officials to have shoddy work passed and approved. There were loud cries of 'Shame, shame; resign!' The Speaker interrupted the leader of the opposition. 'Please raise your question and do not make a speech.' But his order fell on deaf ears. 'We want a full debate on the subject,' someone shouted. 'Crores of rupees of the public have been squandered in bribes. Bridges with substandard material have collapsed. Roads laid by the department are full of potholes after every monsoon and have to be repaired.' The volley of angry complaints turned into a tirade.

The Speaker stood up and said, 'Please, this is

question hour. If you wanted a full debate you should have asked for it.' He called out the name of the third questioner. 'Please, all others sit down.'

But the ministers refused to take their seats. Instead, they stormed into the well of the House waving sheets of paper and shouting, 'Shame! Shame!' in chorus. On his scribbling pad Zora put down the word '*Hijda*' with a smug smile. The Speaker sat down holding his head in his hands. After a while he stood up and said, 'If leaders of opposition parties have no questions, I will go on to the next member. Yes, Mr Zora Singh, raise your question.'

Zora stood up and waited for members of the opposition to return to their seats. He waited till the House was completely quiet. The Rajya Sabha was silent when he began, 'Mr Speaker Sir, I crave your indulgence in allowing me to make a few preliminary remarks before I come to the question under discussion. As you know Sir, most of the accusations made against the Ministry of Public Works deal with construction works carried out during the time when I was chief engineer of the PWD. The accusations being made against the Honourable Minister are in fact directed at me. If there has been any wrong-doing, do not accuse the Honourable Minister who is as pure as the purest gold, but hold me responsible.'

'Indeed! Indeed! You can see all the purest gold on the Minister's fingers,' someone shouted out from the opposition benches. There was a burst of laughter. The Prime Minister had a broad smile on his face. The Minister held up both his hands to let everyone see the gold rings he wore. The House was in good humour.

Zora let the laughter die out and resumed his speech. 'Mr Speaker Sir, and fellow members of this august House, look up and around you. This building was erected before most of you were born. Is there anything wrong with it? Has a single brick or stone come loose because it was fixed in with sub-standard material? Your humble servant was part of the team that built it.'

There was the thumping of tables and cries of 'Hear! Hear!'

Zora continued. 'The two Secretariats, the Rashtrapati Bhavan, the Prime Minister's residence and the residences of the ministers of his Cabinet, the bungalows and flats you occupy as MPs, these were all constructed during my tenure. Have any of

khushwant singh

these buildings collapsed because sub-standard material was used in constructing them? Here I have a sheaf of clippings praising their design and construction. Your humble servant had a hand in their building.'

There was another round of thumping and cries of 'Hear! Hear!'

'What is your question?' demanded the leader of the opposition.

'That, sir, is not for you to ask but the Speaker,' retorted Zora.

The Speaker intervened. 'Mr Zora Singh, you have made your point. If you have no question to ask, please wind up your speech.'

This was not good enough for Zora. 'Sir, my question is not directed to the Minister but to members of the opposition. If you gentlemen wanted information, authentic information of the working of the PWD, you should have come to me and not danced into the well of the House like a bunch of hijdas.'

All hell broke loose. The opposition rose as one and demanded an apology. 'Sir, he has insulted us by calling us eunuchs. It is unparliamentary and should be struck off the record!'

zora singh

The Speaker could not help but smile. 'The honourable member should not use unparliamentary language.'

Zora was prepared. 'Sir, to call a person a hijda is not unparliamentary. There are three hijda members of Vidhan Sabhas. Who knows, in the next elections there may be some sitting in the opposition benches.' Saying this Zora sat down. He knew that what he'd said would put him on the front pages of the next day's papers.

*

Zora was in a mood to celebrate—but not with his cronies guffawing at the way he had snubbed the opposition into silence. He would delay the celebration till the evening, play a round of golf after which he would join his friends at the bar for a drink or two—or three. Then what? Back home to his arthritic wife. Come to think of it, he had not had sex with her for more than ten years. Neither seemed to want it any more. They bonded now over their passion for religion. And Deepo had reconciled herself to being her mistress's companion-cum-ayah. Zora settled for a long siesta and an evening at the Golf Club.

He got home in time for lunch. He looked tired but triumphant. He told Eeshran what had transpired in Parliament, leaving out the ruckus over the use of the word 'hijda'.

'You are looking very tired,' Eeshran said. 'Why don't you rest in your study? Let Deepo massage your feet for a while. You will be able to sleep better. I'll keep the telephone off the hook.'

Eeshran hobbled to her bedroom. Zora washed his face and stretched himself out on the sofa-cum-bed in his study after switching on the AC. He did not expect Deepo to tend to his tired limbs but left the door unlocked just in case she decided to do so. He was half asleep when he heard the door open and shut. Deepo dragged a *moorha*, sat by his bed and began to massage the soles of his feet. It was very relaxing. She moved her hands to Zora's calves and knees and gently kneaded them. Zora spread out his thighs and drew her hand upwards. Deepo stroked his inner thighs and felt his member rising. She pulled down her salwar and straddled him. They lay pounding into each other for a full fifteen minutes till Zora made a few frantic thrusts and lay back exhausted. Deepo slipped out of his study as silently as she had come.

zora singh

Zora slept right through the afternoon till he heard Eeshran enter and call out to him. 'It's evening; don't you want to get up? You must have been really tired.'

'I was,' replied Zora with a big yawn. He looked at his watch and exclaimed, 'My God, it's past five! Too late for golf. I'll take a shower. Order chai.'

Zora went into the bathroom. He felt the stickiness between his legs. He soaped himself thoroughly, changed into fresh clothes and joined his wife in the sitting room. Deepo brought in a tray of tea and samosas. Eeshran asked her, 'Did you massage his feet?' Deepo replied with a straight face, 'He was fast asleep. I did not want to disturb him.'

'Do it now, then,' Eeshran said.

So Deepo massaged Zora's feet while he drank his tea and ate the samosas.

'Have you any programme for the evening?' Eeshran asked Zora.

'I've missed my golf; what other programmes do I have without you? You want to go out for a drive? Or to India Gate?'

'We can go to Gurdwara Bangla Sahib. There is

a very good *raagi* from Amritsar doing the *keertan*. We can stay on till the evening prayer is over. You will like it after the tiring day you've had.'

So the gurdwara it was. Most people in the congregation recognized Zora—they had seen his picture in the papers and on TV. After paying obeisance to the Granth Sahib, Eeshran, assisted by Deepo, found a place to sit behind the raagis. Zora went around the Granth Sahib twice before he sat down on the other side. He did not want to be disturbed. He closed his eyes and was lost to the world. There were only divine words set to divine music sung by a divine voice. They reached home after the evening service. Such was the peace that prevailed upon them that any small talk would have been sacrilege.

*

As Zora had anticipated, his comment on hijdas made the front pages of all papers. There were also laudatory references to his oratory. The telephone rang incessantly. Strangers and friends congratulated him on his performance. Among them was his Minister. 'Zora *bhai*,' he said, '*kamaal kar diya*—you excelled yourself.'

zora singh

'Mantriji, as long as I live I will not let anyone touch a single hair on your head,' replied Zora. 'I hope your enemies are silenced forever and the Prime Minister has realized your true worth.'

'*Dekho*, let's see. As I said before, he lends his ear to all kinds of malicious gossip.'

Zora's six-year term as a nominated member was coming to a close. With it would go the MP's bungalow which had been at the disposal of the Minister, the MP sticker on his car windscreen and all the other privileges that went with being a Member of Parliament. Zora was worried about his future. He went to see the Minister to seek his advice.

'I have been thinking about it,' replied the Minister. 'They are unlikely to give you a second term in the Rajya Sabha. They did give it to some members earlier but later we took a decision that one term was enough, and that others who have distinguished themselves in the fields of art, literature, music, films, social service and other areas should be given a chance. It was a wrong decision because writers and artists take very little interest in Parliamentary affairs, while people like you who have done signal service to the nation and are still active are denied the privilege of continuing your good work. But that's how it is. Do you have anything else in mind?'

'Sir, it is for you to decide my future. Whatever little I have achieved is by your grace.'

'Would you like the governorship of a state? I am sure I could persuade the Home Minister to appoint you. We need to have one or two Sikh governors. And who can be a better candidate than you?'

'That is very kind of you, sir. But a governorship would mean I would have to leave Delhi. I don't think Eeshran would like that. Is there anything else you can suggest which can keep us in Delhi and let me retain the bungalow for your convenience? I am now over seventy, and if nothing else, I would like to leave behind a good name.'

'Zora, don't talk like that,' remonstrated the Minister. 'You will live to be a hundred. Let me think about it. Be assured I will do my best for you.'

'Thank you, sir, thank you. You are my *annadaata*, my provider.'

*

zora singh

Weeks went by, then months. It was Zora's last day in Parliament. Like other members due to retire, he was invited to make his farewell speech. And, as on other occasions, he excelled everyone else even in his farewell address, combining sentimentality with humour. He returned home somewhat depressed. The first thing he did was to order his servant to remove the MP sticker from the windscreen of his car. In a few days he would receive a notice to surrender the official bungalow to some new Member of Parliament. He had never used the bungalow in the six years he had it, but where would his Minister and dear friend go to entertain his lady friends now? Zora was concerned. The man had not as much as rung him up in the last two months. Perhaps he had made some other *bandobast*.

As anticipated, a few days later Zora received a notice to hand over possession of the official bungalow by the end of the month. The same evening his Minister rang up. 'Zora, my friend, I have some good news for you. You will be happy to know that the Cabinet has agreed to honour you with the title of Bharat Ratna, the highest honour the nation can bestow on anyone. With it comes the bungalow. You may hang on to it for the rest of your life. There. Are you satisfied?'

Zora was overcome with emotion. 'Thank you, oh sir, thank you. I thank you from the bottom of my heart. Please give my wife the news, please, could you tell her—' Zora broke down as he handed the phone to Eeshran. He continued to sob, 'Bharat Ratna. Bharat Ratna for poor, undeserving Zora Singh. Blessed be Wahguru. *Dhan Wahguru, Dhan Dhan Wahguru!*'

wanted: a son

Devi Lal was deeply interested in God and religion. As a young man he was obsessed with the problem of existence, and argued with his friends, the pujari of the local temple and the imam of the nearby mosque. Was there really a God, he asked. When assured that there was, he wanted to know if God was truly almighty, all-knowing, just and merciful. When assured that God was all that, he asked, 'Then why is there so much injustice in the world?' He got different answers from different people. Some said that people suffered because of the bad karmas of their past lives. Others explained that suffering was in fact a gift from the Almighty, since those who remained steadfast in their devotion to Him despite all trials were assured of a place in heaven. Yet others maintained that the world was

Maya, an illusion created by God, and suffering, too, was mere illusion. None of these explanations satisfied young Devi Lal. He was more inclined to believe that while God was the power that kept the world going, He was neither good nor bad but supremely indifferent to what happened to individuals—why some were born with brains, enjoyed good health and prosperity and begot sons, while others were born dim-witted or diseased, remained poor all their lives and begot daughters. He was a whimsical God, Devi Lal concluded, a *Vadda be-parvah*, as Guru Nanak had called him—the Supreme One who could not care less.

This was what Devi Lal believed through much of his youth. But by the autumn of his life, he was convinced that God was indeed just and kind, even if his ways were sometimes inscrutable. This is the story of how Devi Lal became a believer.

*

Devi Lal's father taught Urdu and history in a government school on the outskirts of Jalandhar. He was acknowledged as a great scholar of Punjabi history and an honest and upright man, but that did not translate into any riches or professional success.

wanted: a son

He received no patronage from the local princes nor from the British, whom he admired, and was superseded thrice to the post of headmaster. Devi Lal had grown up seeing him struggle to meet the needs of his family of a wife and four children, three boys and a girl, of whom Devi Lal was the youngest. All their relatives were much better off and looked down on them. This made Devi Lal angry with God. But when he himself received a scholarship after his matric examination to go to college, he was willing to give the Almighty the benefit of the doubt.

After graduation from the DAV College in Jalandhar in 1951, Devi Lal got a job as a draftsman in the office of the architect commissioned to design Chandigarh, the new capital of Punjab. He drew a respectable salary of two hundred rupees and worked with Chief Architect Le Corbusier and his assistant Pierre Jeanneret. They only spoke French, which Devi Lal did not understand, but this was never an impediment. They liked his work and often patted him on his back. So did their English colleagues Maxwell Fry and Jane Drew. Jane often remarked: 'Devi Lal is the best draftsman in Shandy Ghaar.' Indian architects agreed with their verdict. Devi Lal got rapid promotions and became the head draftsman by the time he was twenty-six. All this was good; he could not have hoped for better.

A year later he received a marriage proposal. The girl was Janaki, a little too homely in appearance. He was unhappy about this, but acceded to his parents' wishes. Besides, she was the only daughter of well-to-do parents and brought a substantial dowry with her, including a brand new motorcycle and fifty thousand rupees in cash. If someone up there had dashed his hopes of a beautiful life partner, he had also provided adequate compensation. Devi Lal decided this was a reasonable bargain. 'What will I do with a beautiful film star that I can't do with my plain-looking Janaki?' he told his friends. 'She is gentle and obedient. She never raises her voice when speaking to me.'

Devi Lal lived in bachelor's quarters provided by the Chandigarh administration. With his savings and the money brought by Janaki, he was able to buy a plot of land in Mohali, a satellite town being built alongside Chandigarh. At the time, prices of land were low and building contractors were eager to provide material and labour at cost price to people who could help them earn more contracts.

wanted: a son

Jeanneret, who had become a friend, designed a neat three-bedroom bungalow as a wedding gift. The bungalow was ready for occupation in six months. Devi Lal spent the cash remaining from Janaki's dowry to furnish it. He named his home Janaki Villa.

Janaki was proud and happy to be Devi's wife. She kept a good home and was very caring about her husband's needs. As a Hindu wife she never displayed wantonness but whenever her husband desired sex she complied by laying herself on her bed, undoing the cord of her salwar and opening her thighs to him. She did not particularly enjoy sex but had been told by her mother that when her man wanted it she should comply. She had come to him as a virgin and was prepared for the pain while being deflowered; the nights that followed were then easier to endure. She had not been told about women's orgasms and never had one. In the fourth month of her marriage she was pregnant. That was good. She prayed that she would bear her husband a son. She made offerings at the Hanuman temple and asked Bajrang Bali to give her a male child. God gave her a daughter. That was not so good. She felt she had let her husband down. Though Devi Lal had also wished for a son, he consoled Janaki: 'If God in his wisdom has given us a baby girl, it is best to accept her as His gift. I am sure she will grow up to be as sensible and dutiful as you.' They named their daughter Savitri.

Devi Lal abstained from sex for six months while Savitri was being breast-fed and then he could hold out no longer. Three months later Janaki was pregnant again. This time she prayed at the Krishna temple, made offerings to the Lord with the flute, the beloved of cows and milkmaids, to bless her with a son. However, the second child was also a daughter. Janaki felt she had let her husband down again. Devi Lal consoled her again, though with less conviction in his words than before: 'I've told you, Bhagwan decides what is best. A second daughter could well be as good as a second son.' They named the girl Leela.

Janaki was relieved that her husband took it so well. However, she was determined to give him a son. When they resumed having sex, she put more zest into it than she had before. She felt, because her worried mother and sullen mother-in-law told her so, that perhaps she had not kept her husband happy in bed and had deserved the punishment she

wanted: a son

got. So now she would strip herself of all her clothes before she lay down and take her husband in a tight embrace when he mounted her. She would meet him halfway as he pushed into her. And now that she did this, she found that she enjoyed sex as she had never done before. Devi Lal, too, liked the less inhibited Janaki and turned what had till then been a ritual into a sensual feat.

After a few months Janaki was pregnant yet again. This time she decided to seek the blessings of the Sikh God Wahguru who she was told answered devotees' prayers without fail. She was familiar with Sikh rituals, since her parents often visited gurdwaras and had taken her along with them before she was married. She found the hymn-singing very pleasant and the recitation from the holy Granth Sahib more orderly than the clanging of temple bells and the loud chanting of Sanskrit shlokas that no one understood. She visited the neighbourhood gurdwara every day, sometimes accompanied by her husband, to listen to the morning service, *asa-di-var*. Every week she donated eleven rupees to the free *langar* run by the gurdwara.

When her third child was born and she asked the nurse, 'Is it a girl or a boy?' and the nurse picked up the newborn and replied, '*Bibi*, it is a very cute little baby girl', Janaki broke down. This time a bitterly disappointed Devi Lal advised her to simply resign herself to her fate: 'It was written in our stars to have daughters. There is nothing you can do. You cannot defy kismet. We'll make the best of a bad deal.' They named the third child Naina Devi, after the goddess who lives atop a hill.

Devi Lal made his peace with a fickle God. There was no use expecting anything from Him. It would be a struggle to arrange dowries for three daughters. He decided not to take any more chances. In any event, his desire for sex had abated and Janaki no longer encouraged him to indulge in it. Whenever the urge overcame him, she obliged. But he took the precaution of withdrawing as soon as he felt the climax approaching. Janaki never questioned or complained, but he felt constrained to explain, so every once in a while he reminded her of the family-planning slogans broadcast over All India Radio: *Do, ya teen, bas* (Two or three are enough). 'We've had our three, so it is *bas* for us,' he would say. '*Chhota parivaar, sukhi parivaar.* We are a small and happy family.' Devi Lal began to spend more time at work than at home, and Janaki began to make frequent short trips to her parents' home in Chandigarh with the girls. The two of them did not spend as much time together as they used to in the first few years of their marriage.

For eight years Devi Lal restricted sex to once a fortnight—*coitus interruptus*. Then he presumed that Janaki had passed the age of pregnancy and became careless. She was thirty-seven when she conceived for the fourth time. '*Hey Ram!*' she exclaimed. 'What will people say—this *buddhi* goes on breeding! I don't want another child. Take me to a doctor and have me aborted.'

Devi Lal had strong views against abortion. 'That will be murder and I can't have that on my conscience,' he told his wife. 'If I have to marry off three daughters I can as well marry off four.' Then he put the onus on Janaki: 'You decide what you want to do.' Janaki did not have the stomach for it, so Devi Lal braced himself for another blow from the Vadda be-parvah.

This time Janaki did not visit any temple or gurdwara nor make any offerings. Eight months and sixteen days after she became pregnant, her fourth child was born. It was a son. The husband and wife could not believe their luck. That very afternoon,

Devi Lal sent packets of sweets to all his colleagues in the office, his friends and relations. 'Strange are the ways of God,' he said to his wife. 'He never fails to surprise me.'

They named the boy Raj Kumar, the prince. The girls were as thrilled with him as their parents. They rushed back from school to play with him. Every morning Janaki put a large black dot made of soot on his forehead to ward off evil eyes. Every other evening he was taken out to Sukhna lake, and the girls took turns pushing his pram, imitating his gurgles and using baby language to make him smile. Their parents, strolling right behind them, looked on indulgently. They were as happy a family as any in Chandigarh.

God seemed to shower his blessings on Devi Lal's family. The three girls, though no beauties, were presentable, well-mannered and above average at studies. They helped their mother in the kitchen and stitched their own clothes. When Savitri was eighteen and Leela sixteen, one of Devi Lal's junior colleagues who had sons in their twenties came to him with marriage proposals. Besides being a government servant, he owned two provision stores in Chandigarh which were looked after by his sons.

wanted: a son

The girls were married off on the same day that winter. Three years later, a building contractor whom Devi Lal had obliged, asked for Naina Devi's hand in marriage for his son, a young doctor who had just completed his MBBS. Naina had passed her tenth standard and wanted to go to college. But her parents refused to let her. 'What use is college education to girls?' they said. 'It only puts wrong notions in their heads. You don't need to go to college to learn how to look after your home and husband.' So at sixteen Naina too was married off. Devi Lal did not have to arrange for a dowry: he was head draftsman and still had a few years of government service left, and the contractor would need other favours. God was indeed being kind to Devi Lal.

*

By the time Devi Lal retired from service, Chandigarh had grown into a modern city. He had seen its birth in the small rest house in Chandi Mandir where Le Corbusier had made his rough sketches of the new city, its lakes and gardens, boulevards, government buildings and neat colonies. To Devi Lal, Chandigarh was like his own child. He was satisfied with what he had achieved in his profession and looked forward to a quiet retired life.

He was a contented man. His daughters had been married into good families and his son showed all signs of growing up to be an officer in some service or the other and earning enough to look after his family and ageing parents. Devi Lal had spared no expense in giving him a good education. The boy was sent to Chandigarh's most reputed public school, where former royal families had sent their sons. Whenever tuitions became necessary, the best private tutors were hired. After every year-end examination he was rewarded with an expensive gift—a watch, a sports bicycle, cricket gear, and a Yamaha motorcycle in his second year of college in Punjab University.

Raj Kumar excelled in his studies and made his parents proud. Devi Lal loved nothing more than showing off his son to relatives and friends. He was not only a brilliant student but a good athlete as well. While Devi Lal was a man of modest build and average looks, Raj Kumar was six feet tall and powerfully built. He had probably taken after some ancestor of aristocratic stock.

wanted: a son

After college, Raj Kumar sat for the civil services exam. Devi Lal was certain that he would be among the top hundred successful candidates. And he was. He could not make it to the most coveted Foreign Service or the Administrative Service but the rest, like the Police, Revenue, Accounts and Forests, were his for the asking. Ultimately, he took his father's advice. 'No service commands as much prestige as the police,' Devi Lal told him. 'A policeman is respected and feared by all, including politicians and ministers. He may have to salute them for the sake of courtesy but he calls all the shots. And his *ooper ki amdani* is much, much more than in many of the other central services—even a *thanedar* of a police station can make a few lakhs a month if he gets a good *thana* in a locality with a high crime rate.' That made sense to Raj Kumar. He opted for the Indian Police Service. He was built like a police officer and had a fascination for uniforms, so it seemed right in every way. It was a proud moment for Devi Lal's family when Raj Kumar got the letter confirming his selection, with orders to report at the Lal Bahadur Shastri National Academy of Administration in Mussoorie. People, including many Devi Lal did not know, poured in to congratulate him and Janaki. Several of them brought proposals of marriage. Devi Lal thanked them, noted down their names and put them off till the day Raj Kumar completed his training and was allotted a government bungalow. 'This little *jhuggi* is not good enough to receive the bride of an officer of the Indian Police Service,' he told them. 'We will talk about it when the time comes.'

Raj Kumar left for Mussoorie. Devi and Janaki got down to discussing the merits of the proposals they had received for their son. 'She must be from a respectable, well-to-do family of our own caste,' they both agreed. 'She should also be well-educated, modern and good looking,' suggested Janaki. 'No one wants a plain-looking *gharelu* type like me for a wife these days.' Devi Lal poked a finger in his wife's belly playfully and said, 'And she should be able to produce sons. Not like you, one daughter after another.'

'That was God's will. He did give us a son in the end, didn't he?' protested Janaki.

Devi Lal had to agree. Not only had the *Ooperwala* given him a son just when he had lost hope, He had also blessed the boy with intelligence, looks and good fortune. And all this when neither

wanted: a son

he nor Janaki had even prayed to Him!

Devi Lal and Janaki now began dreaming of Raj Kumar's marriage. They would have a grand wedding with the elite of the city invited to the reception; they would put up a huge *pandal* in the open space in front of their modest house. Later, they would rent out their house to a reliable tenant and move into their son's bungalow, to be looked after by a dutiful, enlightened daughter-in-law.

They were in for a disappointment. Six months into his training at the Sardar Patel Police Training College in Hyderabad, Raj Kumar wrote to his parents asking their forgiveness for having got married to a woman probationer in his batch without seeking their permission or blessings. 'We fell in love with each other and could not wait,' the letter explained. Worse was to come. 'She is a Sikh,' Raj Kumar wrote. 'You will like her when you see her. Please send us your blessings. Her name is Baljit Kaur Siddhu.'

That year, fifty candidates had been selected for the Indian Police Service, of whom five were women. During the common training for those selected for the Central Services at the Lal Bahadur Shastri Academy, those of the police naturally grouped together. Baljit was the best looking of the girls. Raj Kumar was the only other Punjabi in the batch, and quite handsome. It was Baljit who started to sit beside Raj Kumar in the classes and the canteen. They went out together for evening strolls. After four months in Mussoorie, they were sent to the Civil Defence College in Nagpur. By then they had started holding hands and kissing. Then followed a six-month course at the Sardar Patel National Police Academy in Hyderabad. Boys and girls were housed in different dormitories. Baljit found a way out of the strict segregation of the sexes. One Sunday she took Raj Kumar with her to the city. She had booked a room for the night in a hotel near the Chaar Minar. They made love all day and night and returned to the Academy the next morning. Their absence from the hostel was reported to the Director.

They were summoned to appear before him. 'You know you can be dismissed from service for breaking the rules of the academy,' he said sternly.

Baljit broke down. 'Sir, we are engaged to be married,' she said with tears flowing down her cheeks. 'If we lose our jobs, we'll be ruined.'

It was the first time Raj Kumar had heard of his

engagement and impending marriage. He nodded his head vigorously to lend support to her plea.

'Have you got your parents' permission to marry?' asked the Director.

'No sir, not yet. We will ask for their blessings after we are married. Here in Hyderabad you are our father, mother—our guardian. We will do as you order us.'

The Director relented. After a pause during which he kept tapping his pen on the glass-top of the table he said, 'Okay, get a marriage licence and I will get a magistrate to perform a civil marriage in the Academy.'

And so, two months later, Baljit Kaur Siddhu and Raj Kumar were pronounced husband and wife. The Director—whom Baljit had begun calling Papaji—and his wife hosted a reception for them in the Academy's dining hall. He also helped them to get their postings as Assistant Superintendents of Police under training in Chandigarh.

The Devi Lals were shattered when they read Raj Kumar's letter. 'Without even consulting his parents! What's the world coming to?' said Devi Lal in anger and grief. 'She's not even a Hindu. How will a Sikh Jatni adjust into our family? Their ways and ours are not the same.'

Janaki, though equally disappointed, consoled her husband. 'What's the difference between Hindus and Sikhs? They are much the same. There are so many Hindu-Sikh marriages. At least she is not a Muslim or a Christian. And she is a Punjabi, not some *kaali-kalooti Madrasan* from the South who cannot even speak our language.'

Devi Lal pondered over her words. Yes, things could have been much worse. If God was testing them again, He wasn't being as cruel as He could get. Devi Lal summed up the argument with one of his favourite proverbs: 'What cannot be cured must be endured.' He wrote back to his son sending their blessings, but with a proviso: 'A civil marriage is not good enough for us. We must have a proper Hindu wedding with a reception to follow. What will our relatives and friends say if we don't?'

A few months later Raj Kumar and Baljit Kaur arrived in Chandigarh by the Shatabadi Express from New Delhi. There was quite a crowd of relations, friends and police officials on the railway platform to receive them. Among them, unknown to Devi Lal and his wife, were Baljit's parents and two brothers who had come from their village to receive her. The two stepped out of the train to be smothered in garlands and embraces. Raj Kumar pushed through the crowd, almost dragging his wife to greet his parents, his sisters and their husbands. He touched their feet before embracing them. Baljit followed his example. Janaki waved her hand over Baljit's head and blessed her, '*Sat putri hoven.*' Baljit burst out laughing, '*Mataji*, one will be good enough for us. I don't think I can handle seven sons. Come, meet my parents and brothers.'

Baljit's father was a retired Colonel. He and his sons, tall and tough—as was Baljit herself—looked after their several farms in the village. They appeared to be much better off than the Devi Lals; they had driven from their village to Chandigarh in a Toyota. 'Let us go to the Shivalik for coffee and get to know each other better,' the Colonel suggested. At the hotel, they talked about the need for a wedding ceremony. 'We must have a proper wedding in a temple,' said Devi Lal. 'We must have a Sikh *Anand Karaj*,' asserted Baljit's mother, 'otherwise our relatives will never forgive us.' Janaki suggested a compromise: 'Why can't we have both? One day *pheras* in a temple; the next day an Anand Karaj in a gurdwara.'

'Why not?' agreed Baljit. 'It will be great fun, one couple getting married three times! Don't you agree, Raju?'

Raj Kumar agreed readily. Dates were settled.

When the bearer presented the bill to Devi Lal, Colonel Siddhu snatched it out of his hand. 'We never take anything from a daughter's home. That is not our custom.'

Colonel Siddhu paid the bill and drove them back to Mohali. 'This is my little *ghareeb khana*,' said Devi Lal. 'I could not afford anything better. Please put your blessed feet in my humble abode.'

The Siddhus were disappointed but did not show it. 'It's a charming little house,' said Mrs Siddhu. 'Big houses can be a headache. If you ask me, I'd rather live in a two-bedroom flat than a haveli with dozens of rooms. You are lucky to be living in a manageable home.'

Mrs Siddhu's tone of condescension left no doubt in Devi Lal and Janaki's mind that as far as Baljit's parents were concerned, their daughter had married beneath their class. This was reinforced further in the styles of the two weddings that followed. The *havan* arranged by Devi Lal in the Arya Samaj Mandir was a modest affair attended by relatives and close friends of the family. The Anand Karaj which took place in the Siddhus' haveli was a grand affair with the entire village, distant relations and friends, some from as far away as Canada and the UK, present. They decked up Raj Kumar in a pink *achkan* and *churidar* and slung a *kirpan* around his waist. He looked regal in his Sikh outfit. There were over a thousand guests at the lunch that followed. In the evening the haveli was lit up with coloured lights. Baljit and Raj Kumar were seated in a new flower-bedecked Maruti gifted by the Siddhus. The rest of the dowry followed in a truck: a colour-TV set, fridge, washing machine and steel trunks packed with clothes for her and Devi Lal's family. When the caravan of cars drove out of the village towards Chandigarh, Janaki asked her husband, 'Where will we put all this stuff in our little house?' Devi Lal waved his hand dismissively and said, 'Not to worry. They have been allotted a bungalow of their own. It has four bedrooms, a drawing-dining room, servants' quarters and a garden with a *maali* to look after it. We are lucky in the match our son has made. We should be grateful to God for the way things have turned out.'

Raj Kumar and Baljit spent their first night after

the Anand Karaj in Janaki Villa. Janaki had strewn rose petals on their bed and filled the room with flowers. She knew the couple must have consummated their marriage in Hyderabad but she wanted to believe that it was in his parents' home that her son deflowered his bride. 'Now all I want is a grandson in my lap,' she told her husband as they retired to bed late that night.

The next morning Raj Kumar drove his parents in his new Maruti to his and Baljit's official bungalow. Janaki was charmed by it and wished she was living there instead of Mohali, infested with parthenium, which gave her respiratory problems. But here Baljit was the boss. She ordered about the servants and constables assigned to them. She took Janaki on a conducted tour of the house while Raj Kumar sat in the verandah talking to his father. 'What will you do with four bedrooms?' asked Janaki timidly. 'One is for us; one for my parents or brothers when they happen to stay overnight; one for guests and one for you and *Pitaji* whenever you wish to spend a few days with us away from the cares of your home,' replied Baljit. Meanwhile, Devi Lal obliquely hinted to Raj Kumar at the problem of Janaki's allergy to parthenium. 'The doctor says she must stay

wanted: a son

elsewhere because there is no cure for the illnesses caused by this Congress Grass or parthenium or whatever. I am looking for a small one-bedroom flat somewhere near Sukhna lake or Chandi Mandir and will let out Janaki Villa.' Raj Kumar did not say anything. It was evident he would discuss the matter with his wife before committing himself. Devi Lal wanted to tell his son a thing or two about being the man of the house but as Baljit's imposing, Amazonian form appeared in the doorway, he knew instantly that his son didn't stand a chance.

Some days later, it was Baljit who drove over to Janaki Villa. 'Mataji, you never told me you were having breathing problems because of the Congress Grass growing all around you. I'm not going to let you stay here a day longer. I will send a truck with policemen to help you pick whatever you want to bring with you. You lock up Janaki Villa and come to our house. You can bring your servant with you; I'll give him a room in the servants' quarters. It will be a great favour, actually. We will be out on duty all day long. You can look after our house for us.'

It was clear to Janaki that she was required to be a glorified housekeeper. Every morning at breakfast she asked her son and daughter-in-law what they would like for lunch and dinner. She watched over them as they ate to make sure they had no complaints. When they returned from the office, often late in the evening, Devi Lal and Janaki sat with them for a while, then retired to their bedroom where they had their early evening meal. Both sensed that their son and daughter-in-law enjoyed a drink or two before dinner but that they would not drink in their presence. From the smell of tobacco that wafted into their bedroom they understood that Raj had taken to smoking. From the lipstick on the butts of cigarettes in the ashtray emptied in the morning it appeared that, though a Sikh, so did Baljit. Devi Lal and Janaki felt that what their son and daughter-in-law did was none of their business. They were in awe of the young couple. Every morning when Raj Kumar and Baljit appeared in their smart khaki uniforms, the sight made old Devi Lal and Janaki sigh with happiness; they looked as if God Himself had made them for each other.

One morning, as the pair left the house to get into the police car with a red light on its bonnet, Janaki noticed how shapely her daughter-in-law was: big bosom, slim waist and large buttocks that appeared to be bursting out of her khaki trousers.

wanted: a son

'She is very *risht-pusht*,' she remarked to her husband, who replied, 'In English they call it sexy. She could bear many healthy children.'

'One or two would be enough,' replied Janaki. 'First a son, then either a son or a daughter. And then full stop.' She laughed and repeated the family-planning slogan that her husband had told her about years ago: 'Chhota parivar sukhi parivar.' She had regained her humour. She breathed more easily.

Raj Kumar and Baljit did not want to start a family right away. They wanted to familiarize themselves with their jobs before having to look after children. So, even after marriage, they continued to use condoms while having sex, as they had done when their liaison started in Hyderabad. After the first few times, it was usually Baljit who took the initiative. She wore knee-length nighties which bared her large, smooth buttocks whenever she bent down, which she did often; her large, firm breasts were always visible through her sheer attire. If that did not arouse Raj Kumar, she demanded a goodnight kiss which she prolonged till he got the message. She was more vigorous than he when they were in the act. He had to quickly fish out a condom from under his pillow and came within a minute or two, leaving her aching for more. She explained to him why she was so randy. 'You see, I am a full-blooded Jatni of peasant stock,' she said to a breathless Raj Kumar. 'You are a city-bred Khatri, of the trading class. We are more lusty than you. In fact, you people cannot beat us at anything physical.' Stung by the comment, Raj Kumar did his best to put more zest into the act. 'I'll fuck the hell out of you, you sexy Jat bitch!' he would shout as he heaved in and out. 'Okay, fuck the hell out of me if you can,' she challenged. He was never able to fuck the hell out of her. She never had an orgasm.

After two years of the couple's posting in Chandigarh and two years of love-making with condoms, the parents on either side started dropping hints about wanting a grandson. At first Baljit put them off with a smile, 'What's the great hurry? We have plenty of time.' But her own mother was most insistent and said to her, 'Young women bear healthy children; middle-aged women's children are often sickly. And if you give your husband a son now he won't stray even when you are not so young. Youth leaves you in the blink of an eye, *puttar*.'

Baljit was persuaded. She put it to her husband.

wanted: a son

Raj Kumar thought about it, then said, 'Why not? If it's okay with you it's okay with me.' He stopped buying condoms. Sex became more pleasurable. Baljit consulted medical books, including one which guaranteed male children if conception took place within certain days after the menstrual cycle was over. She told Raj Kumar about this. He obliged, at times doing his duty four nights running. But nothing happened. Baljit consulted a gynaecologist. She was pronounced fit. 'If you have been taking contraceptive pills or your husband has been using condoms for a long time, it can take a while to conceive. Be patient,' the doctor assured her.

Another four months passed without success. Baljit began to get anxious. Without telling Raj Kumar, she had a seven-day recitation of the Granth Sahib performed at a local gurdwara and made a donation to the free kitchen. It had no effect. Again without telling her husband she had a havan and puja performed at the Krishna temple. This too failed. 'What's wrong with us?' she asked her husband one evening over drinks. 'We have been fucking away like rabbits without contraceptives and yet no *babalog*. I saw a gynaecologist, she said I was okay. What about you?' He replied angrily,

'What about me? I am more than okay. I have a medical test every year. Fit as a fiddle, says the MO.' Raj Kumar had, in fact, already sent a sample of his sperm for examination and been assured that the spermatozoa were alive and kicking, anxious to enter female ova.

Baljit recalled that once they had visited the *dargah* of a Muslim saint in Delhi and seen coloured strings tied around the marble trellis encircling the grave. When Baljit had asked the caretaker what they were meant to be he had explained, '*Mannat*. Worshippers tie these strings as a pledge to give something in charity when their wish is fulfilled. It is usually women who want children who come here. People who are sick also come to be healed and read the *fateha* prayer.' At the time Baljit had listened with a bemused smile on her face. Now she was willing to believe.

There were many dargahs around Chandigarh. Baljit had driven past them but never entered one. There was one on the way to the police training school for junior cadres, on a ridge facing the Mughal Gardens in Pinjore. She was curious about the place as she had seen it grow from a nondescript tomb to one with a neat green dome over it and a

wanted: a son

platform outside with wooden benches. One evening, after inspecting the training school, she asked the driver to pull up outside and entered the mausoleum. A tall young man in a green lungi and kurta and with a shaggy, black beard and shaved upper lip appeared from nowhere and greeted her, 'Salaam, Bibi.'

'Who are you?' demanded Baljit.

'*Huzoor*, I am the caretaker of the *mazaar*. I offer prayers on behalf of anyone who comes to pay respects to Peer Sahib's tomb.'

'Who was Peer Sahib?'

'I don't know much about him, *ji*, except that he was a saintly man and granted the wishes of anyone who came to him for help. I have been newly appointed to this place by the Waqf Board. It pays me very little and this is a very lonely place. Actually, whenever anyone comes here, I get a lot of *sukoon*. Otherwise my heart is troubled. I am thankful to you for coming.'

Baljit looked him up and down. He was a rascally-looking young fellow with thick lips and lecherous eyes. In turn he combed his black beard with his fingers and looked at Baljit up and down, from her cropped hair to her feet, letting his gaze linger at her breasts. 'Bibi, if you wish I will recite the fateha for you, and Peer Sahib will fulfil your *muraad*.'

Baljit nodded. The young man sat down on his knees with his feet tucked beneath his buttocks and raised the palms of his hands in front of his face as if reading its lines. He intoned: *Bismillah-e-Rahman-e-Rahim, Al hamdu lillah Rabbul alameen . . .*' He brushed his face with his hands and asked, 'What is it that you wish for?'

Without hesitating Baljit replied, '*Aulad*, preferably a son.'

The man turned to the Peer's grave: 'Ya Peer! Plead with Allah, the granter of all wishes, to give this woman a son.'

Baljit opened her handbag, fished out a twenty-rupee note and handed it to the man.

'Please wait a minute. You must take some prasad,' he said and hurried to his one-room quarters. He came back with a small newspaper packet. It contained pellets of sweetened rice and sesame seeds. Baljit took it with both her hands, and as she left, the caretaker advised, 'Bibi, if you wish your murad to be fulfilled you should come again to the Peer Sahib to invoke Allah's blessings. And to give this lonely slave of Allah some sukoon.'

Baljit got into her car and told the driver to take her home. She ate a bit of the prasad. It was soggy and oversweet and left a sickly taste in her mouth. She threw the packet out of the car. She did not tell Raj Kumar about her visit to the dargah.

A week later she was back. This time she drove her own car, without the tell-tale red light on the bonnet. The caretaker was delighted to see her. He went over the ritual of reciting the fateha and giving her a packet of sweet rice. This time she raised the offering to fifty-five rupees. 'If my murad is fulfilled, I will offer a lot more,' she said as she left. She put the prasad in her mouth but spat it out as soon as she left the dargah.

The monsoon set in. That year Chandigarh got more than its usual share of rain. Many roads were flooded. Many cars got stuck in knee-deep water. There was not much traffic on the road. Baljit took out her car and told the police driver that she did not want him as she was only going to the neighbouring sector to call on a friend. Rain or no rain, she had to keep her tryst with the Peer Sahib. Driving through the rain, she recalled Shaikh Farid's lines and smiled to herself:

O Farid, the street is full of mud
    And my Lover's home is far away;
If I go my garments will get wet
    It will be false to my Love if I stay;
I care not if my clothes get wet
    It is Allah who sends down rain;
I will go to see my Lover
    Never will I let my Love down, come what may.

The rain intensified. Passing vehicles splattered muddy water on her windscreen. She carried no umbrella and her clothes were wet when she entered the mazaar. There was no one there. She stood at the entrance door and shouted, '*Koi hai?*'

The bearded man's face appeared at the door of his quarters. '*Abhee aaya,*' he shouted back and disappeared again. A minute later he emerged with a gunny sack over his head carrying a packet of prasad in his hand and ran across the open courtyard to the mazaar. 'This is true love,' he remarked as he lowered himself on his knees to recite the fateha. 'The Peer Sahib will surely grant your wishes for coming to him in the rain and mud.'

After the fateha the man handed over the packet of prasad. She gave him a hundred-rupee note.

'Bibi, you better eat the prasad here and let your clothes get dry before you leave.'

Baljit put some prasad in her mouth. It tasted different. She suspected the rascal had mixed something in it. Perhaps a little *bhang*, or maybe opium. She did not care. She began to feel drowsy. 'I feel very tired,' she mumbled. 'Can I lie down here?'

'You may. Some people sleep here all night.'

Baljit lay down near the grave. Sleep overtook her. Sometime later, she felt the man's hands stroke her body. It was a pleasant feeling. She felt his fingers untie the knot of her salwar and pull it down to her ankles. She did not mind. She felt him lift her shirt to her shoulders, undo her bra and take her breasts in his mouth. He sucked like a hungry cub and her nipples went hard. She felt him kiss her all over her face and neck. His beard and the stubble on his upper lip felt good. Then he rubbed and patted her thighs with his rough hands and pushed them apart. She heard a rustle of clothes and felt his hard, heavy body crush hers as he entered her. She had gone moist. His penis was much bigger than Raj Kumar's and kept going in till she felt it was well inside her belly. He moved in and out gently at first and then in a frenzy. She had not known anything like this before. She began to moan and shudder. She had one orgasm, then another. But he had not finished. He came with her third orgasm, grunting softly. He dismounted quickly. In her half-sleep she felt his hands pull up her salwar and re-tie the knot, then adjust her bra and pull down her shirt. She did not open her eyes till half an hour later. 'I fell asleep,' she lied. 'I hope I will be forgiven.'

'Allah is forgiving,' he replied. 'Bibi, I hope I will have your *deedar* again. What you wish for needs a lot of prayer.'

Baljit promised to come back in a few days. She was unsteady on her feet as she got back into her car. Her clothes were still wet. The drizzle had not stopped. She rolled down the window of the car and let the gentle rain fall on her face.

When she got home, Raj Kumar's parents were sitting in the drawing room having tea. '*Beta*, all your clothes are wet. Where have you been in the rain? Change your clothes and have a hot cup of tea or you will catch a chill.'

'The car stalled on the road. I had to get out in the rain to see what was wrong and fix it. I'll change in a minute and join you. Is Raj back yet?'

'He rang up to say he may be a little late,' replied Devi Lal.

Baljit ran up to her room. She shed her wet clothes, dried herself and got into a fresh salwar-kameez. She washed her face in cold water to get rid of her drowsiness, brushed her hair vigorously, put some fresh lipstick on, dabbed her neck and shoulders with eau-de-cologne and joined her in-laws for tea. 'I'll rest a while to get the chill out of my system. Tell Raj to wake me up when he gets back,' she said after tea and went back to her room. She lay on her bed and was soon fast asleep. By the time Raj Kumar came back two hours later she was as fresh as a lotus opening its petals to the rising sun.

She laid out the whiskey. 'I got such a drenching! I need a stiff one,' she said. He poured her a large one and took his usual small peg. The whiskey had never tasted better to her. It warmed her and set up a nice buzz in her head. She felt on top of the world. She was always a cheerful person but rarely as cheerful as she was that evening. Raj Kumar sensed that she would expect him to perform his conjugal duty. He did, and both enjoyed it, more than they had in a long time.

Baljit craved for more favours from the Peer Sahib. She knew she was taking awful risks. There was the CRPF group centre in the valley right across the dargah where junior policemen did their training. All of them recognized her. So did the Punjab and Chandigarh Police. But she was like a tigress who had tasted human blood and thirsted for more. A week later she was at the dargah again. The caretaker saw her pull up her car under a tree where it could not be seen from the road. He quickly got out a board and put it near the door of the little mausoleum. It read in four languages—Urdu, Gurmukhi, Hindi and English: 'The caretaker is on leave for the day. Please put your offerings in the wooden box beside the Peer Sahib's tomb.' He greeted Baljit with an openly lecherous smile: 'Bibi, it has been a long time since you turned your steps this way. I thought you had forgotten your humble servant. Come this way,' he said.

Baljit followed him to his quarters. He unlocked the door and let her inside. All it had was a charpai with a dirty quilt spread over it and a dirtier pillow at one end, a pitcher in a corner with a metal mug dangling on its rim, and an oil lamp in an alcove. There was a window almost at level with the hillside, and a wooden slab to shut it. The caretaker asked Baljit to be seated on the charpai while he shut the door from the outside. He took a lock and key. She heard him lock the door and came back in through the window and shut it. He lit the oil lamp: a faint amber glow lit up the dingy room. Then, without much ado, he sat by Baljit. He took her in his arms and put his mouth against hers. His beard and whiskers pricked her. She pushed him away and said, 'Your hair's so prickly!' He laughed and put his hand between her legs and massaged her crotch. He fumbled with her salwar knot. She helped him to open it and pulled the garment down. He pulled it completely off her legs. She understood and took off her kameez, undid her bra and tossed it to a side. She was stark naked. '*Subhaan Allah!*' the caretaker exclaimed. 'No *hoor* could be more beautiful.' He took off his kurta to reveal a broad and hairy chest, then he undid the knot of his lungi, pulled it off and flung it away. Baljit had never seen a circumcised penis. She ran her fingers over the swollen, smooth head of the long shaft. Without a word, the caretaker pushed her on her back and moved on top of her, resting his hands on either side of the charpai. She threw her legs apart wide and high for him and he slid smoothly into her. 'This is *Jannat!*' he said as he smothered her face with passionate kisses. They went on for more than half an hour till Baljit began to moan. She dug her nails into his scalp and cried, 'You are killing me,' and came. He was bathed in sweat and continued thrusting and pounding till she came a second time and then she felt his hot sperm flood her inside.

He got up, drew water from his pitcher and washed his penis and pubis. She lay where she was without bothering to cover her nakedness. He came and lay beside her. He realized she wanted more and he knew he wanted to give it to her. An hour later she began to play with his penis. He was aroused again. They went through the act a second time. It lasted over an hour till both were exhausted. From the chinks in the door and the window they could see the daylight fading. The caretaker dressed hastily, opened the window and peered outside to make sure no one was about. He jumped out and unlocked the door. Baljit slipped on her clothes and walked to her car. He moved the notice board and lit the oil lamp for the Peer Sahib's grave.

Baljit paid three more visits to the mazaar. She knew that if she did not stop soon, it was only a

wanted: a son

matter of time before someone noticed and guessed the reason. That would be the end of her marriage and possibly her career as well. The last time she went to the dargah, she spent a couple of hours with the caretaker in his dark hovel. Before leaving she sat with him by the grave of the Peer Sahib and while he recited the fateha she prayed for forgiveness. She swore to herself she would never visit the dargah again.

The following month she missed her period.

She did not tell Raj Kumar nor her in-laws. She wasn't sure if she was pregnant, but just to be sure, made Raj Kumar make love to her three nights running.

She missed her second period. Janaki heard her retch and throw up one morning. She asked her directly, 'Beta, are you expecting?'

'I don't know for sure, Mataji. This is the second time I have missed my periods. I will go and see the doctor.'

The gynaecologist examined her and pronounced her pregnant. Raj Kumar was excited at the prospect of having a son: he had been having sex on days prescribed by the medical book which ensured a male child if its instructions were followed to the letter. Baljit abstained from sex after the fourth month of her pregnancy. Although her gynaecologist assured her there was no danger of a miscarriage if she continued having sex for a month or more, she did not want to take any chances. Raj Kumar too had become somewhat complacent as he felt he had done the job expected of him.

It became awkward for Baljit to fit into her police uniform. She applied for six months' maternity leave. The child inside her began to move and often kicked vigorously. She patted her belly gently and spoke to it to be patient.

As the date of delivery approached, Janaki became nervous. She was afraid that history might repeat itself. What if Raj Kumar and Baljit's first child turned out to be a daughter? She told her husband about her fears and wondered if they should perform a puja in the Krishna temple. Devi Lal had been keeping a careful record of the curses and gifts that God had showered on him. All in all, it had been a good life, but now was the time to truly test the Almighty. He wagered: 'I can tell you that God will give us a grandson, regardless of whether we perform the puja or not.'

Exactly on time, at the end of the ninth month,

wanted: a son

Baljit started getting labour pains. Her husband drove her to the maternity ward of the PGI hospital. Two hours later, she delivered a child. It was a son.

Baljit was happy that her visits to the dargah had borne fruit. Raj Kumar and Janaki were thrilled. But the happiest of them all was Devi Lal. He now had no doubt whatsoever that God was merciful.

the mulberry tree

Vijay Lall was an early riser. He awoke to the harsh cawing of the first crows, and when he drew the curtains of his study window, he could see nothing except street lights glimmering in the distance. During the last few mornings of the waning moon, the apartment blocks around the square patch of lawn in his colony were bathed in soft moonlight. Then they made a pleasant sight. But at all other times they looked squat, staid and lifeless, like middle-aged women who had let themselves go. For some years now, the hour or two before sunrise was the only time he could gaze out of his window without being mildly irritated by what he saw.

Facing his window was a large mulberry tree, which had been planted at the time the apartment blocks were built and was over fifty years old,

the mulberry tree

perhaps exactly as old as he. Vijay had developed a special relationship with this tree. Most of the winter it was without any leaves and its dry branches stuck out like the quills of a giant porcupine. During these months only the crows and sparrows visited it. Their cawing and twittering were his dawn chorus. Sometime in mid-February, usually the eighteenth, he noticed tiny green specks sprout from the seemingly dead brown branches. In recent years he had been watching out for this event and noted it down carefully in his diary. A week after they first became visible, the green specks turned into green leaves. And as spring turned to summer, the tree was covered with so thick a foliage that he could not see the branches. It became host to a variety of birds. Even before the eastern horizon turned grey and the call for the *Fajr* prayer floated in from the tall minaret of the mosque across the road, a family of spotted owlets set up a racket—*chitter-chitter-chatter-chatter*—and roused the crows and sparrows roosting there for the night. Then came the green barbets. They wound themselves up with a low *kook-kook-kook* before exploding into an incessant *katrook-katrook*. Most afternoons koels, as shy as barbets, hid behind the foliage and called intermittently till the sun went down and the call for the *Maghrib* prayer rose from the mosque. As it got dark, the spotted owlets set up their racket again, which was a signal that it was time for his sundowner.

The mulberry came into its full glory at the time of the water festival, Holi, in March. Its invisible flowers turned into light green caterpillar-like fruit full of sweet juice. Humans vied with parakeets to be the first to get them. Street urchins threw sticks and stones to knock them down. Within a week the tree was denuded of all its fruit and then all it had to offer man, bird and beast was its cool shade. Stray dogs were chased away by the people living in the block closest to the tree, who tried to grab space under it for their cars against the scorching sun. Since Vijay was an early riser and worked at home, he did not have much problem getting the shadiest spot directly under a huge branch for his twenty-year-old car, a beige-coloured, temperamental Fiat called Annie. Although his car was regularly messed up by bird droppings, it remained cool through the day. It was during the long summer months that Vijay strengthened his personal relationship with the mulberry tree. He

the mulberry tree

greeted it with a 'Hi' when he went to take Annie out for a drive and a 'Cheerio' when he parked her there for the night.

The mulberry tree was a constant in Vijay's life. He awoke to the bird-babble rising from its branches and had his first drink every evening at the hour when the owlets announced sunset. He brought out his woollens when its branches became bare, and began using his air-conditioner when they were heavy with foliage. It was a comfortable, sedate routine.

Then one day the tree almost killed Vijay, and his life was thrown out of gear.

*

It was the month of June; temperatures had soared into the forties. One way of remaining cool was to stay in an air-conditioned room. Another, and a healthier way, was to spend an hour or two in a swimming pool which cooled one off for the evening. Though Vijay felt lethargic after his siesta, he forced himself out of his apartment one particularly hot afternoon and walked to his car under the mulberry tree. It was oppressive and still. Not a breath of air; not a leaf stirred. The sky was a bleached grey. It looked ominously like a lull before a storm. He saw a wall of muddy brown advancing from the west, with kites wheeling above it. At this time of the year, dust storms were common; they blew in and out with blind fury, uprooting trees and telegraph poles and spreading layers of dust everywhere. Vijay thought it wise to get away as fast as he could. He had barely reversed ten yards when a dust-laden gale swept across the colony at devilish speed. He heard a loud crack, like that of thunder following lightning, and the enormous branch under which his car had been parked came crashing down on the tarmac. The earth trembled beneath him.

Vijay switched off the engine and sat still in the car for several minutes. The two chowkidars of the colony ran up to check if he was all right. He waved them away without rolling down his window, and just to prove that he was not rattled, turned Annie around and drove out. His hands were shaking. It was best to be somewhere else for a while.

The storm had blown away as fast as it came. Branches of trees littered the roads. An auto-rickshaw had turned turtle on Mathura Road and a small crowd had gathered around it. Vijay slowed down, wanting to know if the driver had survived, then changed his mind. By the time he got to the club pool, a cool, clean breeze was blowing. For an hour he had the pool all to himself. When other members and their children started streaming in, he came out of the water and stretched himself out on a poolside chair. He covered his face with his bath towel and went over the scene of destruction caused by the storm.

He had had the narrowest of escapes. Instead of being comfortably stretched out on a deck chair, he could have been in the morgue of some hospital with a smashed skull, and every bone in his body broken. What was even more unsettling was the manner in which he had escaped certain death: he did not remember a single day when his old Fiat had warmed up and started in less than half a minute at the very least, but today it had started instantly. A few seconds later and both he and Annie would have been crushed. Was it God's will that he should live a little longer?

Vijay was not sure about God, nor about providence. He had never given these things much thought. Now he did. Half-forgotten stories of providential escape from certain death came to his mind. Some instances that he remembered reading about were extremely bizarre. One was of a plane flying from Dublin to London's Heathrow Airport. It caught fire as it was approaching London. The pilot decided to make an emergency landing on an airstrip near a suburb called Mill Hill. As it descended, the plane hit the chimney of a house and broke into two. All the passengers and crew were killed, except a stewardess who was sitting at the tail end of the plane. She was thrown out of the burning aircraft and into the swimming pool in the garden of the house. Not a bone broken, not a scratch on her body. Why was she singled out for survival, and by whom?

Some years later there was the case of a man standing on the crowded platform of a London Underground station. He fell on the tracks as the train was coming out of the tunnel. The train came to an abrupt halt just as its wheels touched the man's body. The authorities decided to reward the train driver for his vigilance, but he was an honest man and refused to accept the reward. He had not stopped the train, he said; someone in the train must have pulled the emergency cord, though he couldn't imagine why, since no one in the enclosed compartments could have seen what lay ahead on the tracks. Enquiries were made, but no passenger claimed to have pulled the emergency cord. Whose was the unseen hand that had brought the train to a sudden halt in the nick of time? Why had the man's life been spared? Was it to allow him time to finish some task left unfinished? Or was it to compensate him for some good deed he had done?

But the most mind-boggling was a case in Vijay's own country. A man was travelling in a crowded bus along a narrow mountain road. He took a window seat in the last row. Since it was autumn and the weather had turned chilly, he wrapped himself in his shawl and soon fell asleep. He awoke a few hours later when he felt something slimy around one of his ankles. It was a small snake which had found the man's leg a warm place to hibernate for the winter. The man screamed. The bus came to a screeching halt. The driver, conductor and passengers rushed to the back of the bus but shrank back at the sight of the snake curled around the man's ankle. No one had any idea what to do about it. The driver ran out of patience and suggested that the man slowly step out of the bus and sit on the parapet of the road with his leg exposed to the sun. It would induce the snake to leave him and find another dark, warm place and he could then get on the bus following them. The man did as he was told. The bus moved on. The snake behaved as had been predicted: it uncurled itself and slithered down the hillside. The man got on the following bus. A mile or so ahead they noticed the parapet of the road knocked down. The bus ahead of them was lying upside-down in the *khud* at the bottom of the hill. There were no survivors. The only one to escape was the man who had got off the bus because of the snake curled around his ankle.

Vijay went over and over these incidents. He felt disoriented. He left the club as the evening came on. When he reached his colony, he parked his car just inside the gate and walked up to examine the damage the mulberry tree had suffered. The branch which had been wrenched out had left a nasty gash exposing a hollow trunk. The fallen branch had been hacked into pieces to be used as firewood and its leaves stripped off to feed goats. Lots of twigs were littered about the tarmac. No one had dared to park their cars under the tree. Though not superstitious, Vijay also avoided leaving his car near it. He found another place, close to his window. This time the old mulberry tree had failed

the mulberry tree

to demolish him or his car, but he had an uneasy feeling that it had turned malevolent towards him. As he entered his dark apartment and fumbled for the light switch, the strange thought came to him that the tree was in the last leg of its life and had meant to take him with it.

By the next morning everyone in the blocks of flats around the square was talking of Vijay's miraculous escape from what must certainly have been the end of his life. They were used to seeing Annie occupy pride of place under the mulberry tree; they now saw her parked alongside his apartment, without a dent or even a scratch on her body. His neighbours came to congratulate him and get details of the story. With every narration he made it sound more and more dramatic. 'It was the will of the *Ooperawala*,' some of his neighbours said, pointing heavenwards. 'Inscrutable are His ways. If the good lord is your protector, no one can touch a hair on your head.' A silver-haired great grandmother, whom Vijay knew to be close to a hundred years old, added, 'No one can go before his time; no one can live a second beyond the span allotted to him.' Most were agreed that Vijay must have done some good karma in his previous life and had been rewarded for it. God is your protector, they said. God is good and merciful. A faint smile came over Vijay's face at this, as he recalled the lines of a popular film song:

> *Ooperwala*—very good very good
> *Nicheywala*—very bad very bad . . .

It was an absurd song. But what he felt was no less absurd: till this morning he would have described himself as an agnostic; now, though not quite a believer, he felt like God's chosen one.

The morning papers had pictures of the havoc caused by the dust storm on their front pages. A huge neem tree had been uprooted in Chanakyapuri. It lay diagonally across the road and there was a Maruti under it, reduced to a crumpled sheet of metal. Fortunately, there had been no one in the car. A peepal stretched across another road in the Delhi University campus with three mangled cars under it. Four men and two women had been seriously injured and taken to hospital. A small child in one of the cars had escaped unscathed. The storm had taken a toll of five lives: two labourers sleeping under a tree, two cyclists hit by a hoarding

the mulberry tree

which had collapsed on them, and an elderly lady who ran to save her pet Pekinese from a falling eucalyptus only to be crushed under it. Their deaths made news, but among his friends Vijay's narrow escape was the bigger news. They came morning and evening, all with stories of their own: of people who did not get to the airport on time and missed their flights that went down; trains that people had missed that went off the tracks.

The more Vijay heard these tales, the more he was convinced that he was someone special, above the common run of humanity. This added to his state of disorientation, because for as long as he could remember nothing very special had happened to him.

From the block of flats in which Vijay lived, his story spread to the neighbouring Khan Market. The shops were agog with talk of his incredible luck.

Vijay was known to most of the shopkeepers as he was seen in the market almost every evening, peering into shop windows, flipping through magazines displayed on the footpath, going into one bookshop after another and browsing around the shelves but rarely buying any books—they had become too expensive, and, in any case, as a freelance newspaper columnist he got more books to review than he could read. In the two antique shops, he examined figurines of Hindu gods and goddesses, garnet necklaces and brass artefacts, asked their price but never bought anything. In the music shops he hung about listening to tapes being played at the request of buyers. At the greengrocer's he gaped awestruck at monstrous Korean apples, small-sized honey-sweet Japanese watermelons, avocado pears from Bangalore, fresh broccoli, baby corn, asparagus and artichokes. Their buyers were largely European and American diplomats and journalists who in Vijay's opinion drew unacceptably large salaries and spoiled the market rates.

Vijay did not like the shop-owners of Khan Market. They were single-minded in their pursuit of money: everything here was more expensive than in any other market in the city. There were other reasons why Vijay had no time for them. Most shop-owners were Punjabi refugees from Pakistan—in one of his columns he had described them as semi-literate parvenus who had converted their hatred for Pakistan to prejudice against all Muslims. They supported one or the other of the

Hindu fundamentalist parties. Between them they had built a small temple behind the main market which represented their religious beliefs. Ostensibly it was a Krishna temple, Shri Gopal Mandir, named after the deity, and life-size statues of Krishna and his consort, Radha, were put up on the altar. But the temple also accommodated several other deities favoured by the shopkeepers who were masters at hedging their bets. So there was the monkey-god, Hanuman, on one side of the entrance gate and Goddess Durga, astride a lion, on the other. Inside, the left wall had the Sai Baba of Shirdi, with stubble on his chin, one leg over the other and peering into space, and next to him the Sai Baba of Puttaparti with his halo of fuzzy hair and a pudgy hand raised in blessing. There was also a black granite Shivalinga, and in the cubicle next to it, idols of Shiva's consort Parvati and his elephant-headed son, Ganesha. 'To every Hindu his or her own God or Goddess' was the market motto. The only one on whom all were agreed as the supreme divinity was Lakshmi, the Goddess of Wealth.

Vijay did not need the blessings of the many deities housed in the temple, just as he had no need for much of what was sold in Khan Market. The only things he bought were a packet of cigarettes and a couple of *paans*. He put one paan in his mouth, kept another in his pocket to chew after dinner, lit a cigarette and launched upon his hour-long wanderings through the market. When anyone asked him why he made the rounds of Khan Market every evening, he answered, 'To see the *raunaq*. I like watching the happy crowds.' And he would quote the Urdu poet Zauq: 'I pass through the bazaar (of the world)/There is nothing I want to buy.'

There were others who, like Vijay, came to Khan Market every evening for the raunaq of multicoloured lights, fancy cars and trendy people going from shop to shop. Vijay recognized many of the regulars and even exchanged smiles with a few, but rarely spoke to them. There was a woman, in particular, who attracted Vijay's attention and curiosity. She was not a regular but came to the market two or three times a week, not to see the raunaq but to do her shopping. She came in a chauffeur-driven car which was parked at the end of the market, facing the temple. She emerged from the car, always carrying a plastic handbag, crossed the road and went past the temple to another

the mulberry tree

market which had a liquor store. She returned shortly afterwards to dump the bag full of liquor bottles in her car. Then she took out another bag, this time of black canvas, and strolled along the shops at a leisurely pace, stopping at every bookshop window. The only shop she entered was The Book Shop, which was classier than the others and played soft Western classical music at all hours of the day. It warmed Vijay towards the woman, since this was his favourite bookshop too, though he only ever bought his weekly magazines from it. He never entered the shop while the woman was inside. He loitered near the entrance till she emerged, usually half an hour later, and tailed her as she proceeded round the market to the greengrocer's and the butcher's.

When she returned to her car, she handed over the shopping bag to her driver, leaned against the bonnet and lit a cigarette. She surveyed the scene around her as she smoked, unbothered by the looks some of the people coming from the temple gave her. When she had finished her cigarette, she stamped the stub under her sandals—the same bright red pair each time, Vijay had noticed—and ordered the driver: '*Chalo*'. Two doors slammed shut and the Honda City eased out of the parking lot and sped away.

Vijay could not make out why this woman attracted his attention more than other visitors to Khan Market. It was true that he was immediately drawn towards Indian women who smoked and drank: to him, they were liberated women, possibly amenable to entering into frankly sexual relationships, no strings attached. Yet there were several other women he met at parties who also smoked and drank nonchalantly but left no impression on him. What was it about this woman? She had cropped black hair, thicker than any he had seen on another head, and while it was true that he liked short hair on women, that could not be the only reason for the attraction. As for looks, though she had a pleasant face, shapely breasts and an impressive posterior that protruded invitingly, a good number of women who came to the market were better looking.

Why did he follow her around, then? And why was it that he looked forward to seeing her but did not want to get any closer to her and strike up a conversation? It was as if he was afraid of ruining something. His infatuation was a mystery to him. So

the mulberry tree

was she. He tried to guess facts about her life. She usually wore a salwar-kameez, but no bindi on her forehead nor *sindhoor* in the parting of her hair. At first he thought she might be Muslim or Christian, till he noticed she had a *mangalsutra* around her neck. Evidently she was Hindu and married. He could not make out where in India she came from: she could be Punjabi, Rajasthani, from UP or Maharashtra. He gave her names: Usha, Aarti, Menaka. Some evenings, having his drinks, he thought of her and felt warm and mellow. But it never occurred to him to do anything more than follow her around quietly.

A few evenings after the branch of the mulberry tree tried but failed to kill him, things changed.

Vijay saw the woman in the market a little earlier than her usual time. He followed her, as usual, a few steps behind. She went inside The Book Shop. And without thinking about it, he walked into the shop after her. He pretended to browse, picking out a book, reading the blurb, putting it back and pulling out another, as he kept inching closer to her. He heard her ask the proprietress, 'I'm looking for a suitable birthday gift for a boy of fifteen.'

'We have quite a selection for his age group,' replied the young proprietress. The proprietress was a tall and attractive young girl who wore a diamond nose pin. She reminded Vijay of another girl he had known in his youth whom he had wanted vaguely to spend the rest of his life with, but the romance had fizzled out at the prospect of marriage.

'What are his interests?' she asked the woman. 'Stamps, photography, wildlife, shikar, computers?'

'I'm not sure. He reads a bit of everything. Perhaps good fiction . . . about wildlife?'

'What about Joy Adamson's *Born Free*, about her pet lioness Elsa?'

'I think he read that a couple of years back.'

Vijay heard himself say, 'Why not Kipling's *Jungle Book*? It has all kinds of animals: Sher Khan, the tiger, Baloo, the bear. And there is Mowgli, the wolf-boy.'

The woman turned towards him, 'You must be kidding! That is kid's stuff. He read it when he learned to read English.' To soften the snub she beamed a smile at him.

Vijay persisted. 'What about Jim Corbett's books on his encounters with man-eating tigers and leopards?'

the mulberry tree

'He has read all of Corbett's books,' replied the woman, cutting him short.

Vijay did not give up. He was feeling a little reckless. 'I bet he hasn't read Gerald Durrell's *My Family and Other Animals*.'

The girl from the shop lent her support. 'It has long been one of our best-sellers, ma'am. I'm sure the young man will enjoy it as well.'

So it was Durrell's book that won the evening. Both the women thanked Vijay for suggesting it. He felt strangely elated. The woman paid for the book and as she was leaving, turned to Vijay and said, 'Thanks for everything. Goodnight.'

'My pleasure,' he beamed like a schoolboy.

On his second drink later that evening, Vijay found himself thinking of the woman and felt restless. The mellow, quiet feeling of the past had vanished. Had it been a mistake to talk to her? He knew that he could not follow her around silently as he used to. He had crossed an invisible line and now he must get to know her better. He decided that he would do so. He was aware that she must be at least twenty, perhaps twenty-five years younger than him, and he could be snubbed badly, but life was too short not to take chances. The thought of taking chances excited him.

Vijay ran into her again three days later. He was not sure if she recognized him. He took the liberty of greeting her and asked, 'So, how did you like Durrell?'

She gave him a broad smile and replied, 'Hi there! Enjoyed it hugely—both of us. Thanks for suggesting it.'

'You live around here?' he asked. 'I see you almost every other evening.'

'Not far. I like to do my shopping here. I can get everything I want, and it is so cheerful. And you?'

'I live in the block of flats across the road. A poky little flat crammed with books. I have no other hobbies. I'm a boring man. I'll be honoured if you'll drop by some evening for a cup of chai or whatever.'

'Thanks, but not today,' she replied brusquely. 'I may take you up on your invitation some other time. Nice meeting you.' She extended her hand to bid him farewell. It was the first time he touched her. He liked the feel of her soft, warm hand. He wanted to hold it for longer but she did not encourage him. Pulling her hand out of his discreetly, she said, 'See you. I must get things before the shops close.' And she disappeared in the crowd of shoppers.

Another surprise awaited Vijay in his pursuit of his newfound passion. One afternoon he was loitering in the Masjid Nursery looking at plants for sale. There were three such nurseries close to his apartment. Although he bought nothing as he had not enough space in his flat for plants, he liked looking at them, finding out their names and prices. Masjid Nursery, so named because it was next to a mosque, had the largest display of flowers and cacti. While he was going around the nursery, he spotted the woman come to the mosque. She came on foot, there was no sign of her car. She took her sandals off at the entrance and went in. Vijay had assumed that she was Hindu; what was she doing in a mosque? Perhaps he was wrong. But then, Muslim women did not come to pray in mosques. Perhaps her son was at the *madrasa* reading the Quran and she had come to pick him up. Vijay hung around in the nursery for over half an hour. He heard the call for the Maghrib prayer. Men trooped in, taking their shoes inside with them, and fifteen minutes later, streamed out. It began to turn dark. Vijay could not hold his curiosity much longer. He went up to the entrance of the mosque. Only the lady's bright red sandals lay close to the threshold. He peered in. There was a lone man sitting close to the pulpit, reciting from the Quran. To his right was another small door. Possibly she had entered from the main door and left by the side door, forgetting about her sandals. Vijay paused for a few moments, then picked up the sandals and brought them home.

It was a curious, inexplicable sense of triumph—like a scientist making a breakthrough in his research for the lodestone by which base metal could be turned into gold. He now had an excuse to invite her to his flat and get to know her name, to find out who she was and what she did. He put the sandals in a gap in one of his book shelves, next to the leather-bound volumes of *Inferno*, *Don Quixote* and *Rubaiyat* that were his prized possessions. Strange things were happening to Vijay Lall.

The next three evenings he went to the market and spent longer than usual going around the shops. The raunaq of Khan Market was no longer enough. He waited, but there was no sign of her. He bought two packets of cigarettes and a couple of paans. He wandered agitatedly for some time. He returned home defeated.

the mulberry tree

He was luckier on the fourth day. Returning from The Book Shop with copies of *Outlook* and *India Today*, he saw her coming towards him with a bag full of groceries. She was barefoot. Vijay stopped right in front of her and greeted her.

'Good evening.'

'Hi there,' she replied with a distant smile.

'What's happened to your red sandals?' he asked.

She looked down at her bare feet, as if noticing them for the first time, and replied, 'I have lost them. How did you know they were red?'

'I am a very observant man. You must not walk barefoot on these dirty roads and pavements. You might step on a sharp pebble or piece of glass. Surely you must have other footwear at home?'

'Nope. Maybe I should buy a new pair.'

'You can save your money. I have your sandals in my flat.'

She looked him full in the face, visibly alarmed. 'In your flat? Where did you find them? And how did you know they were mine?'

'I am observant and I am also a good spy,' he replied. 'I happened to be in the Masjid Nursery when I saw you take off your sandals and go into the mosque. You probably went out by the side door forgetting about them. I picked them up and took them home. I've taken good care of them. Don't you want them back?'

'Of course I do,' she replied. Her brow gathered in a frown. 'I'll send my driver to pick them up when I'm done with my shopping. Where do you live?'

'No,' he said firmly. 'I will return your sandals only to you and no one else. I've told you, I live just across the road. Besides, you might forget to send the driver. I can tell that you are very absent-minded.'

He half expected to be told to buzz off. But she seemed to like what she heard and smiled. 'That I am. A little off my rocker, as they say. Eccentric and moody.'

'Sounds charming. So, do I have the pleasure of your company?'

She laughed and nodded her head. He accompanied her to her car. She asked her driver to turn around and take her and the sahib to the block of flats across the road. They had no conversation in the car as Vijay kept instructing the driver where to turn to park the car. 'Wait for a few minutes,' she

the mulberry tree

told the driver as they stepped out. Vijay opened the door of his flat and ushered her in.

She looked around the room. 'Books, books, books. You could not have read them all.'

'No, it will take more than a lifetime to read all of them. I just like surrounding myself with books. Do be seated,' he said, pointing to the sofa. 'I'll get your sandals.'

She sat down. She looked sheepishly at her dirty feet resting on the expensive Bukhara carpet. 'I'm afraid I'll dirty your *kaaleen*,' she said.

'Don't you worry about that, it has suffered much worse,' he assured her. 'Stay right where you are, I'll be back in a minute.'

Vijay came back not with her shoes but a basin of water and a towel thrown over his shoulder.

'What's this for?' she asked nervously.

'You'll find out,' he replied. 'See what a mess your feet are—black with gravel and dust. Put them in the basin, I'll clean them.'

A look of alarm returned to her face, but she submitted tamely and put her feet in the basin. The water was warm. He pulled a *moorha* and sat in front of her. 'Relax,' he said gently. She leaned back, rested her head on the blue sofa and shut her eyes. He soaped her feet and sponged them. He took his own time doing this. Then moving the basin out of his way, he put her feet on his knees by turns and rubbed them with a towel. 'Lovely arches,' he said, kneading her feet with his thumbs. 'You may open your eyes. See how clean and soft they look.'

She opened her eyes. She saw the basin full of muddy black water and her feet looking fresh and clean. The thin gold chain around her right ankle was gleaming after the wash. So was the silver ring she wore on one of her toes. 'You seem to be a nice gentleman. But why are you doing all this for me?' she asked. 'I don't even know your name.'

'All in good time,' he replied with a grin. He picked up the basin of dirty water and soapsuds and took it to his bathroom, poured down its contents in the loo and pulled the flush. He washed his hands and came back with the red sandals. Once again he sat on the moorha facing her and slipped the sandals on her feet. 'Don't go about leaving them at the doorsteps of mosques again. They may never come back. Even I might not return them the next time, since they've brought me good luck.'

'What do you mean? What luck have they brought you?'

the mulberry tree

'Made you visit my poky den. I hope not for the first time, or the last.'

She blushed and brushed the hair off her forehead. 'I don't even know your name,' she said, looking straight at him.

'Vijay. And yours?'

'Karuna.'

'Karuna, meaning compassion. A lovely name. But Karuna what?'

'Karuna, that's all,' she said curtly.

'I only asked because I am curious. You have a Hindu name, so what were you doing in a mosque?'

'Nosey, aren't we? Anyway, if it is so important for you to know, I went because I had never seen the inside of a mosque.' She rose abruptly. 'I must go home now. Thanks for everything. I still don't know why you took all the trouble, though.' He walked her to the door. He hoped to linger there a while, to hold her back, but she was in no mood to oblige. 'Bye,' she said without turning back as she hurried away. He heard her car start up and go out of his block of apartments.

An odd character, this Karuna woman! mused Vijay. She was obviously somewhat soft in the head. Or why would a woman who went about in a chauffeur-driven car not buy herself a new pair of sandals and go about barefoot instead? She probably had a well-to-do husband and children. How was it that none of them bothered to notice her waywardness?

More difficult to explain was his sudden desire to get to know her. She was clearly unpredictable—warm and approachable one moment, brusque and distant the next. He would normally not have any patience with such people—he never did, and years of living alone had made him even less tolerant. But despite her erratic behaviour his infatuation with Karuna kept getting stronger. He was not entirely sure of what he wanted: Was he content to just have her around him to talk to and touch furtively once in a while? Or did he want her in his bed for wild sex, the kind he had not experienced in years? All that he was certain of was that the days when he did not see her were unreal and incomplete. Now he found himself thinking: The episode of the lost-and-found sandals must have conveyed my feelings for her. Will she respond?

He went to Khan Market every evening. He pottered around in The Book Shop, looking disinterestedly at new books. He peered inside

the mulberry tree

other bookstores, the grocer's and the butcher's. She was nowhere. Then one evening, for no reason, he went to the Krishna temple at the rear of the market. It was time for the *sandhya* prayer. The scent of *agar* incense floated out of the temple and through the clanging of bells he could hear worshippers sing *Jai Jagdish Hare*! He had never been inside a temple before, or any place of worship for that matter, but something compelled him to enter the courtyard and take a closer look at what was going on. One side of the courtyard was lined with the shoes and chappals of worshippers. A caretaker sat on a stool keeping watch over them. In the second row was a pair of red sandals that Vijay recognized so well. He stayed in the courtyard till the prayer was over and worshippers started streaming out with prasad in their palms. As she stepped out of the crowd, he accosted her.

'What are you doing here?' he asked. 'One evening at a mosque, another evening at a temple.'

'Hi there!' she responded. 'And what are *you* doing loitering outside?'

'I spotted the red sandals but could not steal them. That man with the stick had his hawk eyes on them. So I thought I might wait for their owner and invite her for a cup of tea or coffee.'

'You may not,' she replied matter-of-factly. 'I have another date.' She took a quick glance at her wristwatch. 'Omigod! I'm half an hour late!' She slipped on her sandals and ran across the road to her car.

A month after his miraculous escape from death, Vijay heard of another miracle but did not witness it, though it happened no further from his little flat than Khan Market's Shri Gopal Mandir. One evening when he went there, hoping to run into the elusive Karuna, he saw a long queue, starting at the temple and snaking around the entire market. Everyone in the queue was carrying a tin can, a tumbler, a lota or a thermos flask. He did not like this disruption of the market routine; besides, all these people would make it more difficult for him to spot the object of his affection. He broke through the queue to get to The Book Shop. It was closed for some reason. Disappointed, he walked over to another bookstore, owned by an earthy, robust man who sported a thick, curled moustache, like those worn by men in advertisements for aphrodisiacs. Vijay had named him Hakim Tara Chand. The bookstore owner greeted him affably and as usual asked, 'Some coffee-shoffee, chai-vai?' Vijay waved a 'No thanks' with his hand and asked, 'What is going on here? Who are all those people outside?'

'*Andh vishvas*, sir,' Hakim Tara Chand said, shaking his head but wearing an indulgent smile. 'Apparently the gods are accepting milk from worshippers. Those people are waiting to make their offerings to the idols.'

'What? Stone and metal idols drinking milk?' Already disappointed at not having found Karuna in the market, Vijay sounded more irritated than incredulous.

Hakim Tara Chand was taken aback by Vijay's tone and was apologetic. 'As I said, sir—blind faith. I know you don't believe in these things, nor do I . . . but why deny people the right to believe in whatever they want to believe? My wife went to the temple with a jug of milk this morning and poured it on Ganeshji's idol. The milk disappeared. Where, why, only Bhagwan knows.'

'Good business for milkmen,' sneered Vijay. 'Who started all this?'

'I don't know. But a Hindi paper says that Shreeswamy claims he invoked Ganeshji to accept offerings of milk.'

'Shreeswamy! That crook who has a dozen criminal cases pending against him and has been jailed a few times?'

Hakim Tara Chand put his hands together and replied, 'Forgive me, but I won't say anything against a man who is worshipped by so many—presidents, prime ministers, multimillionaires, film stars. Every other leader of ours goes to him for advice. So I think, there must be something to him . . . Not that I believe in these things.'

'He's said to provide call girls to Arab sheikhs.'

'*Tauba*! Maybe the papers say so. I have no knowledge.'

Vijay sensed Hakim Tara Chand was not keen to talk on the subject, so he moved on: '*Achha ji*, I'll see you soon.' He decided to go back home, but then he thought there might be some chance of finding Karuna at the temple. She seemed to have an unusual interest in places of worship. He didn't think she herself would offer milk as the others did, but she might want to witness the spectacle. So he went along the queue around the corner facing the temple. From the way they were dressed, the people in the queue seemed middle class and educated. Marching up and down, swaying his baton,

the mulberry tree

was a senior police officer in uniform, perhaps a superintendent. There was a large red *tilak* on his forehead, indicating that he had already made his offering. He had four of his constables with him, walking briskly along the queue and asking people not to be impatient. 'You will get your turn,' the officer assured the eager worshippers. 'Be patient, the miracle will go on for some days.' Vijay thought of asking him how he knew, but he did not want to get into an argument with a policeman.

Pye dogs along the queue were licking up the milk that spilled out of the containers. A boy of seven or eight years was warding off a puppy jumping on his leg, wagging his tail furiously and yapping for a few drops. The boy tried to kick the puppy away and spilt some of his milk as he did so. The grateful puppy lapped it up, now wagging his tail in gratitude.

'You can't offer this milk to Shri Ganesh. It has been polluted by a dog,' growled a man standing behind the boy. 'Go and get another jug from the milkman.' The boy burst into tears, poured the rest of the milk on the ground and gave the puppy a vicious kick before going off to look for fresh milk.

Briefly distracted by the commotion, Vijay

walked on towards Shri Gopal Mandir. Three constables barred the way to the road that separated the market from the temple. When those who had made their offerings came out, the policemen stopped all traffic to allow a dozen or so people from the queue to cross the road and enter the temple. Vijay came to the end of the queue. Standing right in front, awaiting her turn to cross the road, was Karuna. She had a large steel tumbler in her hand.

'I had a feeling I would find you here,' he said happily, resisting a strong impulse to reach out and hold her hand.

'Hi there!' she said, genuinely surprised, then looked away. The policemen who had blocked vehicular traffic on the road urged the queue to move on: 'Chalo, chalo, chalo.' About twenty worshippers, Karuna among them, sped across the road to the temple.

Vijay's spirits plummeted as abruptly as they had risen. She hadn't even bothered to wave goodbye, or ask him to wait while she made her offering and returned. Or even suggest that he come with her—it was not the kind of thing he would normally do, but he would have gone if she

the mulberry tree

had asked. He waited for close to an hour to catch her as she came out. Worshippers in the queue kept moving in batches of ten or twenty into the temple and came out with their faces beaming. There was no sign of the one Vijay was looking for. It reminded him of her disappearance in the mosque. She had found another side door.

It was already past his drink hour, a ritual he was very particular about. But today he did not go back home. He looked for her car. The police had ordered all cars to be parked on the road to make room for the crowd of worshippers. The queue seemed unending, as more people kept coming to join it. Vijay walked distractedly through the crowds.

He did not find Karuna's car, so he hung about a paanwala's kiosk, unable to decide what he should do next. His mood had soured. He felt like picking a fight. The paanwala was waxing eloquent about the miracle of the gods to a group of young men in saffron kurtas who were waiting their turn to be served.

'Lalaji, your gods are moody,' Vijay said to the paanwala, 'I have a stone Ganpati outside my flat. I put a cupful of milk to his tusk and his trunk but he did not drink a drop.'

'You have to have faith for miracles to happen,' said one of the young men. 'Faith can move mountains. Lord Krishna held up a hill on his little finger to save his village from a cloudburst. Hanuman uprooted a mountain to get the Sanjeevini herb. So what is unusual about the gods showing their pleasure by accepting offerings of milk from people of all castes, from the highest to the lowest—even *mlechhas*? It is indeed a *chamatkar*.' He looked pleased with his oration.

'This is what makes India great,' added another man. Then he quoted the Urdu poet Iqbal's lines: 'Greek, Egyptian and Roman rulers have all been wiped off the face of the earth; there must be some reason that India still shines in all its pristine glory.'

Vijay felt his temper rise. 'Greece, Egypt and Rome continue to flourish as they ever did in the past; only India remains buried under the debris of ignorance and superstition. Stone and metal imbibing milk is the latest example of our continuing backwardness. This trickery is the best our gods can do!' he proclaimed in a loud voice.

'Stop this *bakwas*!' barked the young man with the caste mark on his forehead. 'If you want to *buk-buk*, do it elsewhere, not so close to our temple. Are you a *Mussalman*?'

the mulberry tree

Soon the argument had become a shouting match. Vijay yelled, 'You are a bunch of *chootiyas*, you make India a laughing stock of the world!'

The young man grabbed Vijay by his shirt collar and shouted, '*Saale*, you dare call us chootiyas! I'll split your arse right here!'

The paanwala jumped down from his seat and separated the two. 'Babuji, don't create a *hangama* in front of my shop,' he pleaded with Vijay. 'Please go home. Here, take your packet of cigarettes. It is a gift from me. May God be kind to you and teach you to overcome your anger.'

Vijay felt humiliated. The boys were almost half his age. He had made an ass of himself by losing his temper.

Vijay had many pet hates, with religious superstition, astrology, horoscopy, numerology and other such methods of forecasting the future topping the list. But mostly he lived peacefully enough with the fools of his world. Even donkeys, he believed, had a right to have their opinions and bray about them. So he was surprised by his outburst at the paanwala's, especially since it had degenerated into physical violence, which he abhorred. He could not understand what had come over him.

He also wondered at Karuna. It seemed strange to him that an otherwise educated, Westernized woman who smoked and drank openly and was seemingly free of religious bias would go about pouring milk over marble and bronze statues, expecting them to drink it up. Perhaps she was doing it for a lark. There was a news item in the papers about two girls who had offered whiskey to Ganpati. There was an uproar and the girls had to beg forgiveness. It was the kind of thing Karuna would do.

After the episode of Ganpati drinking milk and the altercation at the paanwala's, Vijay stayed away from Khan Market for a few days. When he went back, he resolved to walk around the market without stopping outside or entering any shop. He wanted to avoid every place where he might lose his temper with the devout and end up embarrassing himself. He even found a different paanwala for his cigarettes and paan.

On the fourth evening after he ended his short exile, as he was walking past the less-frequented

the mulberry tree

part of Khan Market occupied by a bank which closed its doors to customers, Vijay heard somebody call out, '*Jai ho!*' He turned around and saw a bearded man with long shoulder-length hair carrying a brass plate with flowers, kumkum powder and a tiny silver oil lamp.

'Something for *Shani devta*,' the man demanded, thrusting the plate forward. Vijay realized it was Saturday and the exalted beggar was asking for alms to appease Saturn. There were many others of his ilk around railway stations and bus stands and at road crossings, making money from the gullible. Vijay was not one of the gullible. But what the man said next before Vijay could brush him aside made him pause.

'You have someone on your mind, a young lady may be. So what is the problem? She is not responding, *hain*? I will give you something to win her affections. Close your fist.'

Almost despite himself Vijay clenched his fist and extended his arm.

'Now open your hand,' the man said. Vijay did so. There was a big black ring in the middle of his palm. 'See: it is rahu, the evil planet. I can abolish him. Give me a little *dakshina*, say ten rupees, and I will give you foolproof advice on how to gain your heart's desire.' After a short pause during which the fellow transfixed Vijay with his kohl-lined sparkling eyes, he continued, '*Janaab*, I know you do not belive in *jyotish* or palm-reading. But I can read your face like an open book. Why not try out my predictions and formula for gaining what your heart seeks? Ten rupees won't make you poor nor me rich.'

Without pondering over the matter Vijay took out a ten-rupee note and put it in the man's brass tray.

'Let's sit down somewhere where we are not disturbed by people,' suggested the Shani-man. The only secluded place they could find was a narrow passage between the public lavatory and the market boundary wall. It was malodorous but unfrequented. The man put his tray on the wall, the ten-rupee note in his pocket and asked Vijay to hold out his right hand.

Everyone enjoys being the object of attention. So did Vijay, even when the bearded Shani-man's gentle prodding and squeezing of his palm, as he examined every line, thumb and finger, assumed erotic overtones.

'There are two marriages in your life,' pronounced the sage.

'I had better get started soon. I haven't a wife yet and I'm not young anymore,' Vijay said.

'A man is never too old for marriage and sex,' the sage assured Vijay, then continued, 'I see a large home, double-storeyed and with many motorcars.'

'That's nice to know. I live in a one-room flat and ride a motorcycle,' Vijay lied.

Undeterred, the man went on. 'There is money, lots of money, name and fame.'

Vijay snubbed him again: 'I could do with both. My bank balance is very low and my name is not known beyond my block of flats and this little market.'

'There is also *phoren* travel soon,' the man went on.

'When? Both the American Embassy and the British High Commission turned down my visa applications. Forget about name, fame, money and foreign travel. Can you tell me anything about my present problem?'

'Date and place of birth,' demanded the soothsayer as he pulled a pencil and small notebook out of his pocket. Vijay told him. He drew several lines, parallel and horizontal. He counted on his fingers and inserted figures in the squares and triangles he had made. Then he shut his eyes and pronounced, 'Her name begins with K.'

Vijay was taken aback. 'How did you know?'

'It's all written in your stars. She pretends indifference but she loves you. I will now give you a magic formula to make her hungry for you and you hungry for her.' The man paused and looked meaningfully at Vijay.

'I already *am* hungry for her,' Vijay said impatiently.

'But you must be hungrier, then she too will pant for you without shame. I can guarantee it. For that I charge fifty rupees. If my formula fails, I'll give your money back with fifty from my own pocket. I'll give you my card, with my name and address. If the formula fails, you send me the card by post and I'll come and return the money.' He fished out a grimy visiting card. It had the letter Om on top with a figure of Ganpati beneath and then his name: Natha Singh, World-famous Master of Science of Jyotish, Astrologer, Numerologist, Specialist in Love Potions.

Now that he had let himself in for the hocus-pocus, Vijay said to himself: What the hell, let's go the whole hog. The fellow got the girl's initial right. He may just get her to take more interest in me.

'Okay, here's another fifty rupees, and if it does not work I'll get the police after you. Okay?'

'Okay, janaab, okay. Hundred times okay. My formula is foolproof.' He lowered his voice to a whisper, 'All you have to do, janaab, is pluck two hairs from your *jhaant* and two from her jhaant, mix them up, swallow one pair yourself and give her the other pair to drink up with a cup of tea. Both of you will be on fire. Guaranteed.'

Vijay was speechless. He looked at the Shani-man disbelievingly.

'You doubt my formula?' the man challenged him. He patted his crotch and declared, 'Don't underestimate the power of the jhaant. It is the strongest aphrodisiac known to man.'

Blood rushed to Vijay's head but he kept his

cool. He did not want to create another scene. 'What kind of love formula is this?' he snapped. 'If I could get close enough to pluck her pubic hair, I need no help from *you*. How do I get her to bare her privates before me, anyway?'

'You can do that if you try,' said the Shani-man as he picked up his brass plate and walked away.

Vijay realized it had cost him sixty rupees to learn that he was as big a chootiya as all those people offering milk to the idol of Ganpati. He weaved his way through the closely parked cars to make his way home and walked straight into Hakim Tara Chand.

'You should be careful of charlatans like that man, Lall Sahib,' he said with a chuckle. 'He is not really a sadhu, just a thug who exploits people's weaknesses.'

He had obviously seen Vijay talking to the Shani-man and handing him money. Vijay's ears went red. He felt as if he had exposed himself in public. His humiliation was complete.

Vijay pondered over the events of the past few days and felt very depressed. He described his mood in his diary: 'Pissed off with the world' and then added, 'Pissed off with myself.' Khan Market had lost its raunaq; he avoided going there for another few days. But the itch to have it out with Karuna got the better of him. Did she know what she was doing to him?

After a week, one Saturday evening, he was back in the market hoping to run into her. He went around her usual haunts, the bookstores, the grocer's and the butcher's. She was not there. Ultimately he went to The Book Shop to get his magazines and ask the proprietress if Karuna had been around. He broached the subject very casually. 'That lady who bought Durrell from you, has she been around lately?'

'You mean Karuna Chaudhury? Yes, she came in one evening to settle her account. She said her husband had been transferred to some other city—she did not say where.'

Vijay was lost for words. He took his magazines and slowly walked back to his apartment. He sensed he might never see her again. And the name Chaudhury yielded no clue. Chaudhurys could be found across the country, from Punjab to Assam, down to the Southern states, and they could be Hindus, Muslims, Sikhs, even Christians. The search would be as futile as that of Majnu sifting the sands of the desert to find his Laila. And that was what he felt like—a lovesick Majnu. Which made him an old fool: he was fifty-four. He tried to console himself—that it was an infatuation that would fade away in time. There would be other women. Or there would not.

It was still too early for his sundowner. Nevertheless, he poured himself a stiff one and switched on his TV to divert his mind to things other than a woman who had slipped out of his hands; a woman he should have left well alone. He pressed the buttons of the remote control and tried one channel after another. Nothing held his attention for more than a few seconds. Suddenly the lights went out and the entire complex of apartments was plunged in gloom. The sun had set but through the twilight he could see the outlines of the mulberry tree, already beginning to lose much of its foliage. The sudden darkness prompted a pair of spotted owlets perched on its branches to break into their pointless racket, *chitter-chitter-chatter-chatter.*

*

the mulberry tree

Most residents of the apartment complex slept late the next morning. It was a Sunday. There were only two old ladies out in the lawn when Vijay returned from his walk in Lodhi Gardens. They saw him drive in and park Annie in her old spot under the mulberry tree.

acknowledgements

I wish to express my gratitude to Ravi Singh and Diya Kar Hazra for making my stories more readable than they were.

F/BEAS/2915/08/09